A
RISING
TIDE

THE PORTAFERRY SHOREMEN

J B MCMULLAN

DEDICATION

My great grandfather, Richard McMullan, was a Portaferry shoreman, sailor and fisherman as were most of his sons. With his wife Sarah they had eleven children and lived within the close-knit shore community in Portaferry. This story reimagines life there at that time.

ALL PROCEEDS IN AID OF CANCER RESEARCH

CONTENTS

LOST AT SEA

Lost at sea, I was not found
But yet I am all around.
I am the Sea though how I fought her,
I'm the sun's reflection on the water.
I'm in that place between sea and sky,
You hear me in the sea-gulls cry.
I'm carried on the salty breeze,
I am the rustle in the trees.
I'm in the passing of the moon,
I am the whisper in the dunes.
I'm in that place between sea and land,
I'm in a thousand grains of sand.
I walk along the frothing foam,
I am the gravelled cry for home.
I'm somewhere on the far horizon,
And always in your thoughts arising.
I move between the passing ships,
With salt sea air I kiss your lips.
But for me, please do not weep
I'm in that Heaven in the deep.

1 BOBBY

The old chapel in the lee of the Windmill Hill seemed to fit perfectly into its setting. It was bordered on two sides by golden gorse bushes and with the backdrop of Lough Cuan and the Mourne Mountains in the distance it was a piece of heaven on earth. Bathed in the autumn sunshine of a Sunday evening it exuded a serenity and peacefulness in keeping with an ancient place of worship. The Holy Hour, that had been passed down through the years and generations, was coming to an end as the chapel doors were opened and the final hymn wafted out on the breeze. Even the birds seemed to stop and listen:

Tantum ergo Sacramentum
Veneremur cernui:
Et antiquum documentum
Novo cedat ritui…
A-A-Amen.

The chapel-goers dispersed in two main groups those going over Tullyboard to the High Street side of the town and those winding their way back down towards the shore.

"The Lord knows I don't mind the Holy Hour but the Holy Hour and a Half is taking it a bit far. I've Paddy's dinner on low and God knows what it'll be like!"

Bessy Murray was giving-off amongst a group of women wrapped up in coats and scarves despite the pleasant weather. These were the shore women who always expected the unexpected. Life was tough at times and, despite Bessy's misgivings, they gained considerable solace from their chapel attendance as indeed had their mothers and grandmothers before them.

Bobby let his mother go on ahead with the other ladies as he drifted into the churchyard and stopped at a grey weathered gravestone. Hesitantly, he read:

In Memory of Captain Robert Gibson
Who Died At Sea on 1st January 1800
Erected By His Wife Martha.

This was his father's grave but as his body was never recovered it was only a memorial. The ship owner had given his mother a small compensation payment which she used to erect the headstone. They were hard times and she could have been doing with the money, but she thought it better to erect the headstone and have somewhere to visit, rather than hopelessly looking out over the Lough for the rest of her life. It was nearly forty years ago but the loss was still lamented by his mother:

"What a start to the New Year, the New Century and you newly born. How could it have happened? He had been to America and back, Australia and the West Indies. A wee jaunt to Liverpool with a cargo of coal, 'I'll see you in a couple of days,' he said, and I never saw him again and he never saw you. Mind you, I can see him yit coming over the Kilbrae with his kit bag over his shoulder - my heart's broken Bobby."

He had heard her say those words hundreds of times and it upset him each time to see her upset. He bit his lip and tasted the salt air. That was his father kissing his lips his mother had told him as a child. He believed it and still did as in essence Bobby was still a child. Medical opinion was that Bobby was 'feeble-minded' in local terminology he was said to have 'a wee want in him' or that he was 'a wee bit saft.' However, those that knew Bobby better were more of the opinion that he was 'not that saft!'

While Bobby would never have the ability to master navigation and be a sea Captain like his father he was still instinctively good around boats and on the Lough. He never went to sea as his mother couldn't bear to let him go after what had happened. Still, he picked up odd jobs at the fishing, lobster creels and trips as far as the Isle of Man and earned a few shillings. It delighted him to come home in the evening and slap his earnings down on the table:

"I'm the man of the house now, Mammy," he would say.

"Ah, indeed you are son, I don't know what I'd do without you," she would reply.

Bobby had only a vague concept of money but as everyone knew that he gave every penny to his mother he was never underpaid for his work. In fact, it was often the opposite as it was seen as a way of indirectly supporting his widowed mother. He had a distrust of paper money, he would rather have ten shilling coins than a ten bob note. He liked to jingle the coins around in his pocket, flick a coin 'head or tails' in the air, see the silver shine in the sunlight and, most of all, he liked the sound of it on the kitchen table, paper money could do none of those things.

"I'm the man of the house now father I'm looking after Mammy," he whispered to the headstone.

"C'mon Bobby we're going to Hannigan's."

Some of the men who had stopped for a smoke outside the chapel were heading off and had given him a shout. One thing about Bobby's state of mind was that he could easily be distracted and the thought of a bottle of stout in Hannigan's allowed him to instantly escape from his maudlin thoughts.

"Ah tell ye this," said Bobby as he joined the men, "there's nothing like the Holy Hour to give ye a thirst. The candle-wax, the incense catching the back of yer throat and all that Latin singing – 'Tantum ergo Sacramentum.'"

The men around him laughed not at him but with

him. The close-knit shore community had thrown an arm around Bobby and his mother since the death of his father who had been a highly regarded and respected figure amongst them.

As the group of men sauntered leisurely towards the shore they were silhouetted against a sun-set sky of turquoise-blue and gold. It was so common place that they never lifted their heads from their pipes and their talk. Bobby watched mesmerised, he knew that the sun was going to bed somewhere behind Killyleagh, as his mother had told him that in a story many years ago.

Suddenly, there was the alarm-call of a blackbird in the hawthorn hedgerow which Bobby instinctively answered. The men continued on their way without taking any notice as they were all aware of Bobby's ability to imitate bird-calls.

As well as messing about on boats as a boy Bobby also spent hours rambling through Nugent's demesne. He would lie in the long grass at the top of the Walter Meadow for hours watching the clouds race across the sky and listening to the birds. He started to imitate their calls and they would answer back. 'The birds talk to me, Mammy,' he would say, and his mother would smile thinking it was another one of his childish affectations.

As it turned out it was not a misspent youth but time well spent as it proved to be rather lucrative to Bobby in later years. The monotony of many a long winter's night in Hannigan's was often broken by

Bobby doing his bird impressions: the corncrake, curlew, lark, gulls, oyster catchers, which always ended in rapturous applause and a couple of bottles of stout heading in his direction. Invariably, someone would shout:

"Hey Bobby, if ye were a bird I wouldn't like to clean yer cage!" and Bobby would return a two-fingered salute in the direction of the voice.

He was also in demand from the local Gun Club as his calls could bring the birds onto the guns. A good day at the shooting and he would be rewarded with a brace of birds or, failing that, a few shillings for his efforts. To put a duck on the table for Christmas dinner was his absolute delight:

"I'm the man of the house now, Mammy," he would say after a successful day's shooting.

"Indeed ye are son, sure Ah don't know what I'd do without ye." Everything was right in his world heading off to midnight mass with the prospect of roast duck for Christmas dinner and supper as well.

The walk to Hannigan's took him past his own house at the shore. It was one of the old fishermen's cottages right on the shore front. There was a small porch that opened directly into the living room and just off the living room was his mother's small bedroom with a rather dismal view of the backyard. A hallway leading to a narrow galley scullery was where a set of wooden stairs could be pulled down to give access to Bobby's attic bedroom.

There was no running water. In the corner of the

scullery was a white enamel bucket that Bobby filled with water from the street pump. This was supplemented by rain water that was collected in a big wooden barrel in the yard. A set of steep steps led from the yard to the outside dry toilet. It was all very basic and rudimentary and was the same in all the old cottages at the shore front. The view looking across the Lough was Heaven but the living quarters were far from Paradise.

Bobby opened the door and saw his mother boiling a kettle on the big black range in the living room:

"I'm just going up to Hannigan's, Mammy."

"Do ye want a drap o'tay before ye go, the kettle's near boilt and I've some warm soda bread here that ye like?" The thought of warm soda bread with melted butter momentarily tempted Bobby:

"Och sure I'll get it when Ah get back."

"Well take a coat with ye, the sun's gone to bed and it'll be caul' when ye come out."

Bobby slung the coat over his shoulder and hurried to catch up with the men further up the street. His mother watched from the door, she knew Bobby's limitations, but also knew that there was no more loving son in the whole of the town or country for that matter. She returned to the fireside and poured her tea thinking that his father would have been proud of him.

2 HANNIGAN'S

Being a Sunday evening Hannigan's, of course, wasn't open and anyone contravening the licensing laws would be prosecuted and the owner could lose their licence and livelihood. The men diverted up the loanen that led to the back fields behind the shore cottages and which also led to Hannigan's back door. A special knock on the door saw it quickly opened and the small group of men just as quickly admitted. Only Hannigan's regulars knew the sequence of knocks that would gain admittance and it was changed every now and then to keep one step ahead of the authorities and avoid detection.

Hannigan's was a spirit-grocers occupying a two storey dwelling at the top of the Kilbrae. Tommy Hannigan and his wife lived above the pub on the ground floor. From his bedroom window Hannigan had a perfect view of the Lough right up to the Narrows which was the point where Lough Cuan got into a fight with the Irish Sea. This battle created turbulent and swirling waters known locally as the Routen Wheel. When coupled with low lying rocks and pladdies it was one of the most notorious parts of the coast for shipping and many came to grief at that point.

Hannigan had a collection of old ship's binoculars and a telescope that had come from ships that had foundered in that particular area. He used them now to keep a watchful eye on all the comings and goings up and down the Lough and, more than once, had been the first to report a ship in difficulty.

Although he now ran a pub his hardened, weather-beaten features portrayed a man who had spent a lifetime at sea. That was until his boat came in and went down just off the Rocking Goose near the Narrows. It was a foul night with a south-westerly gusting to gale force. The crew had taken to the life-boats and had made it safely into Quintin Bay.

Meanwhile, Hannigan had taken to his boat and made it safely to the sinking ship. To board a sinking ship, when the rats were quickly leaving it, was extremely risky if not foolhardy. But fortune favours the brave and Hannigan made his own fortune from being the first man on board.

Only a few people knew exactly what he got from the wreck but in the weeks afterwards he travelled back and forward to Belfast before announcing that he was retiring from his life at sea and opening a pub. In essence what he got from the wreck was 'Hannigan's Spirit-Grocers.'

At the time there were about thirty pubs in Portaferry, every street had a pub and every pub had its own clientele. Hannigan's catered for the hardworking, hard-drinking shoremen. Maybe it was working in the salt air all day or spending long periods at sea but these men could drink well into the early hours of the morning and still never miss an outgoing tide. And they could do the same the next evening and the next, as a result, Hannigan's was open all hours every night of the week.

The pub itself seemed to be a depository for Hannigan's maritime collections. There were ships bells, clocks, barometers, brass lanterns, sextants, glass buoys, books, paintings, more binoculars and a couple of cannon-balls warming themselves by the fire. Behind the bar was a fine mahogany ship's wheel which was said to be from the Eagle's Wing that went down in 1715. Just inside the front door was a rather colourful ship's figurehead of a scantily clad female, it can only be hoped that the ship plied its trade in tropical seas rather than arctic waters.

Whilst Hannigan had given up his maritime pursuits he still did a bit of wheeling, dealing and concealing. As regards the latter, a part of the main room of the pub was sectioned off with floor-to-ceiling mahogany panels. Unsurprisingly, they had been salvaged from a wreck and legend had it that they had been bound for a Viennese ballroom. They now shared a space with perhaps a less genteel audience but if they could talk Hannigan would have been sunk. He had employed a ship's carpenter to fit concealed hinges to one of the panels. When the wrong knock came to the door or the authorities insisted on admission, the customers would quietly lift their drinks and smokes and retire to the 'backroom' which would then be locked from the other side of the panel.

Hannigan's was known to have the best wine and spirits in the town and at the lowest prices. The two don't add up unless they are brought in tax-free from the Isle of Man or salvaged from a sinking ship - which they were! The 'backroom' was used to store such goods or if any of the lads had salvaged goods but needed time to negotiate with buyers Hannigan allowed them to be kept there for a small percentage of the profits. The authorities knew what was going on at Hannigan's but could never work it out. And so Hannigan continued to sail in calm waters content in the fact that he no longer needed to make a living from boarding sinking ships. Instead of braving storms he could now, in some comfort, watch the sun sink into the Lough in the evening before going to bed somewhere behind Killyleagh, as Bobby would say.

The door was quickly locked behind the small group of chapel-goers which drew a puff of smoke from the fire. When it cleared Bobby saw his two mates Mucker Mulligan and Captain Rogers sitting in their usual positions on each side of the fire. Mucker had taken his boots off and was warming his feet on the cannon balls which absorbed the heat from the fire like a hot iron.

"Wud ye look what the wind's blown in," said Mucker.

"Where were ye 'til this hour?" asked the Captain.

"Sure it's Sunday night wasn't Ah at the Holy Hour," replied Bobby.

"Och is yer Ma still making ye go to the chapel?" jibed Mucker.

"My Mammy doesn't make me do anything, I'm a man now Mucker!"

"Ah, if ye didn't get up the road to the chapel sure she would give it to ye along the back of the legs," continued Mucker.

"Indeed she would not, my Mammy never touches me," retorted Bobby.

"Ah, that's where she went wrong, the sally-rod across the broad of yer back when ye were younger would have done ye no harm."

"A good punch in the gub would do you no harm Mucker!"

"Well any craic out the road, Bobby?" said the Captain interrupting the usual fond greetings passing between Mucker and Bobby.

"Nah, Ah was just saying that the Holy Hour gives ye a quare thirst," said Bobby, looking hopefully to

Mucker and the Captain but getting no response he continued:

"That incense gets right to the back of yer throat and all that Latin singing: 'Tantum ergo Sacramentum..'"

It has to be said that Bobby's singing was not quite as good as his bird impressions and before he could start another verse the Captain gave Hannigan a nod and a glass of porter magically appeared.

"Cheers Captain, Cheers Mucker," and their three glasses clinked and reflected in the red glow of the fire. The door was opened again and from out of another puff of smoke Paddy Murray appeared.

"Did ye get yer dinner, Paddy?" asked Bobby.

"Aye, but sure Bessy was that long at the Holy Hour the mate was as dry as a camel's arse. I taul' her I'd have to go up to Hannigan's to cure me druth. It's an ill wind as they say Captain."

"Indeed Paddy, I could tell ye all about an ill wind."

Paddy quickly moved on not wishing to listen to another one of the Captain's epic maritime tales.

"We're for the Isle of Man in the morning Bobby, first tide so don't be late," said the Captain. Bobby was too busy drinking to answer but as he was never late he didn't need to reply.

Most of the shoremen worked in small crews of two or three at the fishing, crabs, clams, lobsters, a bit of 'this and that' or just whatever they could make a living at. The Captain, Mucker and Bobby were a tight crew known jokingly as the brains, the brawn and the bammy. The Captain's nautical knowledge was unsurpassed, Mucker provided the muscle and most thought Bobby was 'a wee bit saft.' However, the Captain was one of those firmly of the opinion that he was 'not that saft' and considered him a valued member of the crew.

He could handle a boat and read the tides as well as anyone and perhaps more importantly he picked up information from everywhere. Folk tended to talk in front of him thinking he wasn't listening or that he wouldn't understand. He heard where the fishing was good and other crews would be surprised to find the Captain had got there before them, when they thought that only they knew the favoured spot. He would engage the police Sergeant in friendly conversation and find out when he would be taking a holiday or a short break and when the coast would, therefore, be clear. Invariably, he was always among the first to hear of a ship going on the rocks and would have the boat ready for the Captain to go before anyone else. Mucker and Bobby had grown up together and he was also of the same view as the Captain as regards Bobby.

3 THE CAPTAIN

Captain Rogers or simply, the Captain, as he was generally known had been a good friend of Bobby's father. They were both sea Captains and they had spent a short time together in the Navy. When Captain Gibson was lost at sea the Captain made sure that Martha and Bobby were looked after and provided for. And since retiring as a sea Captain he had taken Bobby under his wing and really treated him like his own son.

He was now in his sixties and often said that, in his time, he had sailed too close to the sun and as a result his skin was the colour of teak and as tough as the leather on a cow's backside. His white beard and shock of white hair, plus the fact that he had only one leg and used a crutch, gave him the overall appearance of a salty old sea-dog.

He was known for having an iron-like grip and could arm-wrestle any man in the town into submission regardless of their size or age. Although he was retired as an ocean-going sea Captain and had a small naval pension, salt water was in his veins and, therefore, he continued to work on the Lough. He was fond of saying that he had sailed the seven seas and had fallen into all of them but he was more wary of the Lough than any of them.

The Captain had been in every port you could think of and many more that you had never heard tell of. Whenever a young mariner turned up in Hannigan's, having returned from some far flung destination, the Captain was always able to converse with him in some detail about the best eating and drinking places and the people who lived there. One remarkable story was when a young sailor returned from Rio and sought out the Captain:

"Captain, you'll never guess who was asking for ye, an old friend of yours in Rio – Zuki!"

"God bless us all is he still alive? Has he still that oul' yawl we made about forty years ago?

"He has, but he's not fishing anymore, he's using it as a hen-house in the back garden."

"Are ye going out there again?" enquired the Captain.

"Aye, in a month's time," replied the young mariner.

"Well, will ye go to the yawl and at the stern look to see if there's a penny squeezed between two of the planks. I put it there as a 'luck penny' when Zuki and I built the yawl. Ask him if you can return it to its rightful owner."

Months passed until one evening the young man came into Hannigan's. The Captain was sitting by the fire with his back to him.

"Hey Captain, there's yer penny!"

When the Captain turned round the young man flicked the coin in his direction and the Captain caught it with one hand.

"Jesus, would ye look at that!" said the Captain with the penny in the palm of his outstretched hand. Everyone gathered round to look at this old blackened penny that had been half way round the world and back. It was incidences like these that gave the Captain an authenticity and standing in the shore community. He was a natural story-teller and as with all good story tellers there was usually some embellishment of the facts. But no one doubted that he had sailed the world and a great amount of truth was embedded in his sea tales.

Bobby loved the stories. He liked nothing better than to be sitting by the fire in Hannigan's with a bottle of stout and the Captain relating one of his old maritime tales. One story that no one believed, except Bobby, was about the time the Captain got swallowed by a whale. In trying to escape the Captain got stuck in the blow-hole until eventually with the build-up of pressure he shot out like a cork from a bottle. At this climax to the story Bobby would jump up out of his chair simulating the Captain's release, shouting:

"Good on ye Captain, good on ye!"

And for the rest of Hannigan's regulars Bobby's antics turned out to be the most entertaining part of the story.

A more plausible story was how the Captain had lost his leg. Although it had gained more layers in the telling and retelling over the years', the fact that he had left Portaferry with two good legs and returned with only one, was sufficient corroborative evidence that the story was to a large extent true. The Captain always started the story in the same way:

"Sure the last time I saw my left leg wasn't it high kicking its way round Cape Horn.

"Now Cape Horn is a very dangerous place. It's where the Atlantic Ocean meets the Pacific and it makes the tussle between Lough Cuan and the Irish Sea seem like a fart in the bath.

"I was skipper of a fine old barque, the Jasmine, with a heavy cargo of timber. The hold was full and it was piled up on the deck as well, so we were already riding low in the water.

"Mind you we had a fair wind and we flew past the Galapagos and Easter Island in good time, only two days out of Ushuala port, when the fair wind turned to foul. The wind increased to Force 10 but the Jasmine seemed to be riding it out until a rogue wave as high as the Windmill Hill hit us midships.

"I saw the pile of wood on deck shifting but Ah

couldn't get out of the way in time. My left leg was trapped and Ah shouted to the ship's carpenter to cut me free. He started sawing the wood but the ship started to list badly and was going down. 'You'll never get through the wood, cut my leg off, I yelled at him!'

"He looked at me in disbelief not sure what to do, so I grabbed him by the neck and shouted 'ye cut it or we're both going down!' He did as he was told this time and we were both thrown into the water as the Jasmine disappeared.

"There were planks of wood everywhere and Ah grabbed one and hung on. The cold salt water seemed to numb the pain in my leg and Ah was washed up on a beach at Ushuala days later – the only survivor."

The Captain always paused at this point to great dramatic effect, 'some good men lost,' he would say as he blessed himself, blew his nose and wiped a tear from his eye before continuing:

"It must have been nearly a week later that Ah woke up in hospital with a young doctor called, Mossie, sitting by my bedside smiling at me.

"Is there something funny, Ah said, Ah've lost my leg ye know!"

"Yes, but losing your leg saved your life, he said, and look at this. He then produced a crutch that he had carved out of the plank of wood that saw me to shore. 'Black ebony,' he said, 'very tough wood.' He then turned it round to show how he had painted exotic dancing girls down one side and we both fell about laughing.

"After that we became very good friends until eventually Ah was fit enough to board a ship heading homeward."

At this point the Captain would hold up his black ebony crutch complete with the colourful dancing girls. From their state of dress it seemed likely that they were related to Hannigan's ship's figurehead. When Bobby got a porter too many he would often stare at them mesmerised as they appeared to him to be actually dancing. But there would be no dancing tonight as it was an early start in the morning for the Isle of Man. The Captain and Mucker drank up and Bobby followed. "See yis in the morning," said the Captain.

"Aye, aye Captain," replied Bobby, saluting the Captain, before hurrying home for his soda bread and tea.

4 MUCKER

Next morning Bobby's mother was up early and generally fussing around:

"I've buttered two soda farls for yer lunch Bobby and there's buttermilk in the tin caddy."

Bobby didn't hear her from the scullery and she didn't look for a reply as she scurried about. His mother was always nervous when Bobby was going on the Isle of Man trip and she would have the rosary beads on the go until he returned. She went out to the half-door to have a look at the Lough.

Being a shore woman she knew the run and turn of the tide and could tell how the weather was likely to fare from the gathering clouds and wind direction. This particular morning God in Heaven couldn't be looking out on a better day and this set her heart at ease. There was a gentle breeze in the right direction that would be good for the sailing. Crimson flakes of mist wavered on the breeze and the low beam of the sun sparkled the Lough with a million diamonds in a molten sea of silver. The Lough was so smooth it seemed almost possible to just walk across to Strangford. She was so entranced by the scene she was startled when Bobby put his hand on her shoulder:

"I'll see ye this evening," said Bobby, "it looks like we'll get there and back by midnight."

"Here, take yer lunch," said Martha handing Bobby a biscuit tin, "there's a couple of soda farls in there and buttermilk in the caddy. Bless yerself and do as the Captain says."

Bobby blessed himself from the holy water fount in the porch and headed up the street. Further along the shore he gave Mucker's front door a rap and he came out almost immediately:

"Alright Bobby how's yer mother?"

"She's grand she worries about me ye know."

"Ah, sure she's nothing to worry about today, I could take my trousers off, hoist them to the mast, and they'd take us all the way to the Man.

"Aye, yer big fat-arsed trousers could do that alright," laughed Bobby as he ran on up the street to avoid a swipe from Mucker. They were still exchanging insults and laughing when they reached the Slip. The Captain was already on board:

"That's what Ah like to see," said the Captain, "a happy crew's a good crew."

"Happy!" said Mucker, "Ah think we'll leave him in the Isle of Man, Captain."

"Ah, ye don't mean that now," said the Captain.

And he didn't, Mucker was dying about Bobby, and anyone trying to belittle him or make fun of him, had Mucker to contend with and Mucker was not one to be contended with.

The Captain's boat was a clinker built cutter. It was one of the fastest boats on the Lough and with the Captain at the helm and his knowledge of the winds and tides it was, in fact, the fastest. He hadn't bought the cutter but had found it adrift just over the Bar at the mouth of the Lough. With Mucker's help he had got a line on it and brought it ashore at Bankmore. No one knew where it had come from but it was thought that it may have been a Revenue cutter that had lost its moorings on the Night of the Big Wind. These type of vessels were built for speed and were widely used by the Revenue men to try and control smuggling that was rife around the coast at that time.

The Captain wasted no time in disguising the boat's origins and converting it for his own use. Its name-plate "The Oyster" was quickly removed and the cutter was repainted in black tar. The Captain was fond of remarking that 'looking for a black boat on a moonless night was like a blind man in a dark room looking for a black hat that wasn't there.' In exchange for a bottle of whiskey another shoreman Jack Tomelty painted a new name-plate – "The Auld

Dog" - in shiny red lettering. 'The Auld Dog for the hard road', the Captain was also fond of saying, and Bobby would invariably add, 'Aye, and for the rough sea as well, Captain,' not really understanding how a boat could be used on the hard road.

For what the Captain had in mind for the Auld Dog required another bottle of whiskey and a complete re-fit by a handy carpenter. When finished it had a false bottom, stern and bow, in reality, it was now a boat within a boat. While it had plenty of deck space these areas, in particular, would be used to conceal contraband. The Captain was joining the small band of smugglers that operated in and around the area.

He didn't like the term 'smugglers' and preferred to be referred to as a 'free-trader,' in explanation he would contend:

"If a man wishes to sell me whiskey or rum at a certain price what business is it for the Government to increase that price with excise-duty? It's like income-tax. I remember that being introduced and my Da saying that the Government would never put its hand in a man's pocket and take the few shillings that he'd earned. Well, look how that turned out!"

Except for his spell in the Royal Navy, it should be said, that the Captain had never paid income tax in his life and he was not going to break the habit of a life-time now by paying duty on alcohol or tobacco.

The band of smugglers were made up of fishermen and ex-sailors who knew the Lough and sea as well as they knew the back loanen to Hannigan's pub. They were better sailors than the Revenue men and their intimate knowledge of all the inlets around the coast usually enabled them to evade capture when pursued.

A favourite spot was east of Wolf Rock at Kearney where there was a gap through the rocks that led into a cave. When being pursued by a Revenue cutter they seemed to magically disappear into the rocks and the larger cutters couldn't follow them or risk getting too close to the rocks. They also knew that the Revenue men were very wary of the notorious Bar Mouth that had claimed many ships over the years. The smugglers could negotiate this area with their eyes closed and on a dark foggy night they may as well have had their eyes closed. Once they reached this point from across the Irish Sea they knew they were safe as the Revenue men would exercise discretion rather than valour and would turn back towards safer waters.

Smuggling or 'free-trading', as the Captain preferred, was not viewed as criminal activity within the wider community. It was seen as a way of evading the Government's greed and allowing poor people the opportunity to purchase goods at a price they could afford – free-trading in other words. The smugglers were popular figures and were readily assisted by locals in landing and concealing contraband. For the popular figures of Mucker and Bobby the Isle of Man trip was a welcome change to the usual work on the Lough and they were in buoyant mood as they loosened the ropes and jumped on board the Auld Dog.

They were on an ebb tide and very quickly were passing Bobby's house at the shore front. His mother was out with the holy water to give them a blessing as they passed. The Captain and Mucker waved towards her and Bobby stood up waving both hands energetically. Mucker put his hand in the water and, unnoticed, sprinkled some salt water to Bobby's face causing him to bless himself.

"By God, Bobby, yer Ma can fairly fling that holy water away out to us here in the middle of the Lough."

"Ah know, must be the wind catching it," replied Bobby still waving.

The Captain and Mucker smiled at one another as they tacked and the Auld Dog gathered pace with the wind in her sails.

They were soon approaching Rock Angus that lay in wait for unwary shipping half-way between Killard Point and Ballyquintin Point. After the loss of the Eagle's Wing in 1715 a thirty foot, white-washed beacon was erected on the rock but with no light and so ship wrecks continued to happen. The Lough at this point was only navigable with care on its eastern side, the western channel was shallow and rocky and the graveyard for many a ship.

"Are they still talking about putting a light on that thing?" said Mucker as they entered the eastern channel.

"Aye, and Ah hope they just keep talking," said the Captain,

"Why's that?" asked Mucker.

"Well for a start, if they put a light on it we would never get a bit of plunder from a wreck ever again and the Revenue men would be on our tails right down to Ballyhenry Bay."

"Ah, when you look at it like that now Captain you've a fair point," concluded Mucker.

They were now passing close to a small colony of grey seals sunbathing on the rocks. The Auld Dog had alarmed them and they were calling out with Bobby mimicking their calls.

"They're giving us a cheer, Bobby," said the Captain.

"Do ye think there's any seal people among them?" said Bobby, "their eyes look like sad people's eyes."

"Could be Bobby," continued the Captain.

"Do ye think they could swim as far as Liverpool?" asked Bobby.

"They could get there quicker than us," replied the Captain.

Staring at the seals, Bobby fell silent, the Captain knew he was thinking about his father and the stories that seals could take on human form from the souls of lost seamen, so he quickly changed the subject.

"Well Mucker how's Mary Ellen?" asked the Captain.

"Ah, she's grand," replied Mucker.

"And how's aul' Dan?"

"He's grand as well," said Mucker glumly.

Mucker had been courting Mary Ellen Mawhinney now for over twenty years but her father was against the match. He vowed that if Mary Ellen married Mucker he would leave the small family farm to his nephew Nigel. Mary Ellen loved the farm as much as she loved Mucker but the thought of her feckless cousin, Nigel, getting their farm swung the balance in favour of not marrying until after her father had died. Her father was an elderly gentleman but to Mucker's misfortune he enjoyed fairly good health. This turn of conversation took Bobby's thoughts away from seal people and sparked an outburst of singing:

> Oh love is pleasing and love is teasing
> And love is a pleasure when first its new
> But as love grows older then love grows colder
> Until it fades away like the morning dew.

Mucker was about to grab Bobby but couldn't help laughing when the Captain joined him in the next verse:

> Oh love and porter makes a young man older
> And love and whiskey make him old and grey
> But what cannot be cured must be endured
> And now I am bound for Amerikay.

"Hey, that's a good idea," said the Captain winking at Mucker, "hoist the main sail Mucker and we'll head for America."

"We can't do that Captain," said Bobby beginning to panic.

"Indeed we could Bobby, I've been there many a time. I'll tell ye this Bobby there'd be no soda bread for yer lunch ye'd get a steak the size of a cow's arse."

"I like soda bread," said Bobby, "and anyway my Mammy wouldn't know where I was and she'd be worried about me."

"Ah I'm only joking Bobby," said the Captain.

Bobby turned his back on Mucker and the Captain, in a huff, opened his biscuit tin and started to eat his soda bread in a defiant manner. The Captain again winked at Mucker:

"Ye know Mucker a bird I love to hear is the curlew, its call is like music in the air, I love to hear it."

"Sure Bobby could do a curlew even better than a curlew," said Mucker.

"Could ye Bobby?" asked the Captain.

While some people claimed to be able to 'whistle and chew meal' there was no chance of imitating the curlew and chewing soda bread. So Bobby put the farl back in the biscuit tin, drank some of his buttermilk, and the beautiful call of the curlew rang out. And almost immediately the call was answered by a curlew on the near shore.

"By God Bobby ye could charm the birds out of

the trees," said the Captain.

Feeling rather pleased with himself Bobby turned to face Mucker and the Captain who was equally pleased at how he had cleverly got Bobby back on side.

Talk of Mary Ellen and her father had Mucker thinking and he sat staring pensively out to sea. He was a powerfully built man, not tall but not small, he had thick thighs and broad shoulders and could carry a bag of coal on each shoulder as if they were feather pillows. Bobby was also right about the 'fat-arsed' trousers. His parents had died when he was still young and he was reared by his grandmother at the shore. And she had done a good job, as despite his tough exterior, he was mild-mannered and particularly respectful and helpful to all the old people he had grown up with. He knew that wee Winnie Watterson who lived next door to Bobby loved crab meat and he threw her in a few cribbens every week. He carried water, chopped wood and lit fires for those unable to do this work for themselves. In short, he was well liked by everyone but, of course, most of all by Mary Ellen.

Mucker and Mary Ellen had been childhood sweethearts but were now both past the first blush of youth. Initially, he had got on well with her father and regularly helped out on the farm. He still helped Mary Ellen to get the cart loaded up for the monthly market in the Square where usually she sold butter, eggs, a few chickens and various vegetables.

Her father owned a small farm out at Marlfield where the fields swept down to the shores of Lough Cuan. It was once a larger farm that he worked with his brother John but when John died his half of the farm went to his son Nigel, who now worked independently of his uncle. Mucker had often enjoyed working at the harvest with Mary Ellen bringing the lunch out to the workers in the field. They would sit at the top of the field watching the Lough flow by and talk about their plans once they got married. Since the incident with the cow they now did more watching than talking.

Mary Ellen's father had a small dairy herd which was his pride and joy, and the pride of the herd was his prize Friesian whom he had named 'Catherine the Great.' An incident with any other cow and Mucker may have been forgiven but not with Catherine. It was a cold February night, dark and wet, and Dan was out in the barn where Catherine was calving. He called for Mucker's assistance when he realised that the calf was coming the wrong way. Mucker, as always over eager to help, reached inside the cow and pulled with such force that the calf and the cow's innards spilled out onto the straw. Catherine gave a few gulps of breath and died on the spot.

"Holy shit Mucker! That's no way to calve a cow, you don't know yer own strength, you've killed Catherine!"

Mucker was dumbstruck, he would never harm any animal and his feeble words:

"I think the calf's alright…" hung in the night air as Dan, inconsolable and distraught, at the sight of his prize cow lying dead at his feet stormed out of the barn and up to the farmhouse. Mary Ellen came running out and Mucker was still standing there in disbelief at what had just happened. Mary Ellen was also visibly shocked at the sight before her.

"Mucker, I think ye should go home now. I'll speak to you tomorrow when we get things sorted out."

The news on the morrow was not good. Her father had branded Mucker a fisherman and not a farmer and never wanted his help on the farm ever again. It was at this point that he vowed if Mary Ellen married Mucker while he was alive that he would leave the farm to his nephew Nigel. This was many years ago now and it was only recently, with age catching up with him, that he had relented to allow Mucker to help Mary Ellen with the heavy lifting and getting things sorted for market. But he was under strict instruction not to go anywhere near the livestock.

Needless to say, with the Captain at the helm, the story had taken on mythical proportions in the telling and retelling in Hannigan's. The Captain had entitled the tale as 'Catherine the Great meets Ivan the Terrible.' In his version Mucker as Ivan the Terrible had reached inside the cow and thought he felt the calf's ear and started to pull. As it turned out it was not the calf's ear but the cow's tongue and the story climaxed in the punch-line:

"By God, didn't he pull the cow's tongue out of its own backside!"

At this Bobby would be on the floor laughing and Mucker after twenty years was only now beginning to find the tale mildly amusing.

"A penny for yer thoughts Mucker," said the Captain.

"Ah, there're not worth a penny," replied Mucker.

"Not even my lucky penny?" continued the Captain.

"As the song says, Captain, what cannot be cured must be endured," concluded Mucker.

At this the Captain left Mucker to his thoughts as he tacked the Auld Dog into the wind and they were effortlessly skimming over the Irish Sea towards the Isle of Man. The Captain was in his element. He had sailed bigger boats on bigger seas but the cutter tearing across to the Isle of Man was always exhilarating. The sun was dancing on the water and the salt sea spray on his face was refreshing. For the Captain the journey was always better than the arrival. He was at ease on the sea and perhaps more so since losing his leg and having to use a crutch. An old sea-shanty came into his head and he gave it full voice on the morning air:

In South Australia I was born
Heave away, haul away
In South Australia round Cape Horn

Bound for South Australia.

Haul away, you rollin' King
Heave away, haul away
Heave away, oh hear me sing
We're bound for South Australia.

Mucker and Bobby were soon lustily joining in on the 'heave away, haul away' chorus. A seal popped its head up to see what all the commotion was about, and seemed to raise its eyes to heaven, as it popped back down again to the more peaceful deeper waters.

The Isle of Man had become the centre for the smuggling trade in the previous century. It was independent of English customs and it deliberately set its own rate of duties lower than England to encourage the trade. It was soon like a vast warehouse importing goods from France and Holland and then being reshipped by the 'free-traders' to various destinations in Ireland and Britain.

The main trade was in tobacco, teas and spirits and they were still the commodities that the Captain dealt in. Eventually the English Parliament bought the Rights to the Island, levelled up the rates of duties and so put an end to smuggling – or so they thought. But old habits die hard and the contacts that had been built up over years continued. The ways and means of getting cheap goods were maintained providing you knew a man, who knew a man and you knew not to ask any questions.

The Captain's man in the Isle of Man was Steady Eddie, sometimes referred to as Unsteady Eddie due to his habit of getting drunk on a Saturday night and falling into the sea, so far, without any fatal consequences. The cold water seemed to sober him up immediately and he just got himself out, got himself home and dried out at the fire while nursing a hot whiskey. The Captain always gave him the grander title of Steadward Edward. Eddie answered to all names but answered no questions – none asked and none answered.

5 STEADY EDDIE

As the Captain started into the twentieth verse of South Australia, most made up and most unrepeatable, the Island came into view. The Auld Dog ignored the main port and seemed to know the way to the secluded bay where it drifted close to the shore-line and alongside a small wooden jetty. Eddie was already there and Mucker and Bobby threw him the ropes.

"Alright Steady?" shouted Mucker.

"Aye, grand Mucker and how are you Bobby?

"I'm good, Steady."

"And yer mother?" continued Eddie.

"She's good too. She gave us a blessing going up the Lough and we must have come across on angels' wings as we were going a dinger."

Eddie laughed, "Ah she's a grand lady, Bobby, and

no mistake. And she's a grand boat yis have now, too."

The Captain, a bit stiff from sitting throughout the journey, got himself out onto the slipway:

"Well Steadward, isn't that a fine day, sun, sea and wind what more could ye ask for?"

"Indeed Captain, it's Heaven sent. And the better the day the better the deed."

The Captain and Eddie stood on the jetty discussing the deed and the deal while Mucker and Bobby made their way towards an old black-tarred fisherman's hut just above the high-water line. The Captain liked dealing with Eddie as he was an ex-Portaferry man and could, therefore, be trusted. 'There's too many thieves in this business' he would say without a hint of irony. Eddie had married an Isle of Man girl some forty years ago and had lived there ever since. He enjoyed the Captain and others coming over and keeping him up to date with the news from home.

Meanwhile Mucker and Bobby had made it to the fisherman's hut to survey the business of the day. It was packed with French brandy, bales of tobacco and a number of tea-chests.

"A bit of heavy lifting there today, Bobby," said Mucker.

"Aye there is, Mucker" said Bobby more interested in the sand martins coming and going from the huge sandbank behind the hut.

"Well Bobby have ye inspected the cargo, I hope

everything is ship-shape?" said the Captain as he and Eddie approached the hut.

"Ah couldn't really say Captain until Ah get a drap o'tay and maybe a wee drink and smoke afterwards.

"By God yer not a bit saft, Bobby," said Eddie as he went into the hut and lit the primus stove to get the kettle on the boil.

Outside the hut was a large ship's mast that had been washed up from a wreck many years ago and was now used as a seat along the front of the hut. On a winter's day they would all be huddled round the stove inside the hut but today they were sitting outside warming their backs against the blackened side of the hut that was radiating heat. Eddie soon emerged with four tin mugs of steaming hot tea.

"Ah hope that's to yer satisfaction, Bobby," said Eddie.

Bobby was too busy getting his soda bread out to answer. Mucker was also unpacking his lunch of thickly buttered wheaten bread that wee Mrs Watterson always baked for him. 'The best wheaten bread in the town,' Mucker would say, knowing the more he praised it the more he would get. The Captain was more exotic in his choice of lunch, two hard boiled duck's eggs and cold boiled potatoes which he salted liberally.

"Would ye take a duck's egg, Steadward?" asked the Captain offering Eddie one of the boiled eggs, "Mucker gets them for me from Mary Ellen's and they're fresh as they were still in the duck's arse yesterday."

"Ah tell ye this, Captain, Ah haven't had a duck's egg in ages, they keep more hens here than ducks," said Eddie readily accepting the Captain's offer.

"How's Mary Ellen and aul' Dan, Mucker?" asked Eddie.

"Both grand Eddie," replied Mucker.

"Ye know," said Eddie winking at the Captain, "I think Dan's father lived 'til he was ninety-six, aul' Dan will probably live to be a hundred!"

"Do ye think so?" said Mucker glumly.

"Well what about aul' Ned," said Eddie changing the subject, "is he still playing the fiddle?"

"Och indeed he is. He was in Hannigan's last week and the place was jumping. Bobby was up dancing around the flure," said the Captain.

"Call that dancing," said Mucker, "I mind cutting the head off a rooster at Mary Ellen's one Christmas and it ran round the farmyard with no head and it made a better shape at the dancing!"

"We should maybe cut yer head off Mucker and see how you get on," said Bobby in a quick response.

"Do ye still do the arm-wrestling Captain?" said Eddie opening another line of conversation.

"Ah wud if I cud but there's no takers anymore," said the Captain.

"Tell ye what," said Eddie, "there's a tavern on the other side of town there and they would bet on two rats running up a wall. Next time yer over pay them a visit and ye'll redd up."

"I'll keep that in mind," replied the Captain.

"Ah hear aul' Sergeant Berry's retired," continued Eddie.

"Aye, retired and living in Church Street now," said the Captain, "he was one of the best. A bit hard on the boys with no lights on their bikes but left us boys in the boats alone. Sure wouldn't he come into Hannigan's on a Sunday night and with a wee brandy on the house he was as quiet as a mouse."

"What's yer new man like?" continued Eddie. The Captain spat on the ground before answering and Eddie sensed an unease between Mucker and Bobby.

"Sergeant Fecking O'Neill," the Captain replied, "a land-lubber from land-locked Tyrone and his side-kick Constable Fecking Rogan is not much better.

"They're the opposite of Berry they don't bother with the bikes but bother us in the boats. They've got themselves a patrol boat and knowing nothing about the Lough they'll either kill themselves or kill us!

"And ye know what Steadward," the Captain was now really getting into his stride, "as well as Sergeant hasn't he also taken up the post of Receiver of Wreck!"

"The Lord save us," said Eddie, "sure there hasn't been a Receiver of Wreck in Portaferry for years. Ye have to be a despicable sort of a man to want to deprive poor folk of a few odds and ends of a wreck."

"Yer right there Steadward. Once ye know that the crew's safe why should we not help ourselves to a few bits and bobs rather than watch them sink to the bottom of the sea. Ye might get a medal for saving the crew but that doesn't put a smoke in yer pipe or a drink in yer glass!"

"Well Bobby we may get this stuff shifted," said Mucker knowing that the Captain would go for some time about the new Sergeant.

Bobby and Mucker started to carry the contraband down to the slipway. When they had it all stacked up on the jetty Mucker jumped on board the Auld Dog and Bobby handed him in the various goods. Mucker carefully packed them in ensuring that the weight was evenly distributed across the boat. It was a task he took time with as incorrect loading could cause a capsize in bad weather although the weather was unlikely to be an issue on this trip.

Meanwhile the Captain's volcanic eruption on his least favourite subject had burned itself out and Eddie and him had lit their pipes and returned to the usual topics of old friends and old times. Bobby joined them, finished off his buttermilk, and wiped his mouth on the sleeve of his jacket.

"Ah tell ye, Bobby, that buttermilk's the boy to put hairs on yer chest," said Eddie.

"That's what my Mammy always says," replied Bobby.

"And have ye hairs on yer chest, Bobby?" continued Eddie.

"Nah, Ah don't even like buttermilk," said Bobby.

"Ah ye see, if ye wud listen to yer mother ye wud have a chest on ye like the Captain's beard."

"Ah'm not sure I would like that either," said Bobby, "anyway we're all ready for inspection, Captain."

The three of them made their way down to the jetty where Mucker was still on board double-checking that everything was properly stowed away.

"She's as neat as ninepence, Captain, as neat as ninepence," said Eddie, "only that she's sitting low in the water sure Ah wouldn't know ye had a load on at all."

"Ah had to use three of the sinkers, Captain," said Mucker.

The Auld Dog carried six sinker kegs. These were weighted kegs where contraband could be stored and could be easily jettisoned if pursued by the Revenue men. They would immediately sink to the bottom but could be retrieved at a later time when the coast was clear. Even if smugglers were caught with sinker kegs on board they would use the argument that they had dredged them up from the bottom while fishing. As there would be no evidence to the contrary such cases never came before the Courts, the kegs would simply be confiscated, and the smugglers were free to ply their trade another day.

"Fine job lads," said the Captain, "we'll have a wee farewell drink with Steadward and be on our way."

They made their way back to the old hut, Eddie went inside and returned with something a bit stronger in the four mugs.

"Your health and safe voyage!" toasted Eddie,

raising his tin mug.

"And keep her Steady Eddie on Saturday night," responded Mucker raising his.

"Ye know Mucker ye don't get any wiser when ye get older," laughed Eddie.

"What about a song Eddie to send us on our way?" suggested the Captain, Eddie needed no encouragement, he had put the following words to an old Irish air:

I wish I was in Portaferry
Only for nights in Ballyhenry Bay
I would swim over the deepest ocean
To see Lough Cuan wind its way...

Eddie was misty eyed when he had finished and his rendition got Bobby's full approval: "Good on ye, Steady, good on ye!" The tin mugs were drained and they made their way back down the beach to the jetty. Mucker and Bobby jumped on board as the Captain exchanged a few last words with Eddie before joining them. Eddie untied the ropes and they drifted away from the slipway:

"Tell yer mother I was asking for her, Bobby," shouted Eddie.

"Ah will," came the reply. Eddie watched until they were a speck on the horizon. He returned to the hut and poured himself another brandy and wistfully started to hum 'I wish I was in Portaferry,' he always felt nostalgic after a visit from the Portaferry boys.

6 THE NEW SERGEANT

Out on the Irish Sea the Portaferry boys were settling into the journey home. The sun was now low in the sky and they would be chasing it all the way to the Port. This was the Captain's favourite time of the day to be sailing. The sun playing on the water in front of the boat, as it faded they would be silhouetted against the evening sky, until eventually, the black boat in the black night would sail silently like a ghost ship, unheard and unseen.

Mucker and Bobby were making the best use of the evening light and had cast their long lines of up to thirty feathered hooks. They were pulling in mackerel, cod, gilpin and a few dog-fish which were generally used to bait the lobster creels. The mackerel and cod could be sold and many locals preferred the gilpins. They each had their own set of customers that they supplied each week.

The banker had a liking for rock-codling but being a bank-manager he was thrifty enough with his money. It was soon discovered that whereas he would pay Mucker or the Captain half-a-crown for a couple of codling Bobby was always better paid with three bob or even two florins. And so the banker had become Bobby's customer. In fact, he usually dealt with the bank-manager's wife, who loved to hear from Bobby where the fish were caught, how fresh they were and how they should be cooked. Bobby knew that the longer the chat, usually the better the money, and he wasn't that 'saft' to miss that opportunity.

The fishing was good and the three empty sinker kegs on the Auld Dog were filling up nicely. By the time they reached the Bar Mouth the moon had taken over duty from the sun. The Captain preferred a moonless night but still they were nearly home.

"Still no light on that thing!" joked Mucker as they passed Rock Angus. The Captain's gaze was fixed in the mid-distance:

"Well here's a light coming," he replied.

A small flickering red light could be seen some way off coming up the Lough. They all knew that this was Sergeant O'Neill in his new patrol boat.

"Awfully dacent of him to shine his red light to let us know he was approaching," laughed Mucker, "will Ah get rid of the sinkers Captain?"

"Nah, just top them up with a lock of fish," said

the Captain as he prepared for the Sergeant to come alongside. It should be said that it was the Captain's skillful maneuvering that brought both boats together as the Sergeant's seamanship was non-existent. They exchanged the usual greetings:

"Evening Sergeant, Evening Constable."

"Evening Captain."

The Captain always enjoyed this exchange as it established him as the highest ranking officer and it seemed to unnerve the Sergeant. Although the Captain was highly critical of Sergeant O'Neill it was perhaps not totally unwarranted as, in person, the Sergeant exhibited no redeeming features.

He had wispy ginger hair, pale-faced with sharp features and eyes that looked everywhere but never eye-to-eye. Despite his position of Sergeant his voice carried no authority and was actually irritable to listen to, although the Captain never listened to it for any length of time, if he could help it.

Mucker actually found his side-kick Constable Rogan just as irritable if not more so. 'Too smart-assed and lippy' was Mucker's assessment and he barely hid his contempt for him. Bobby, on the other hand, tried to rub along with everyone and was his usual cheery self with both of them.

Before taking up his position Sergeant O'Neill had a hand-over meeting with old Sergeant Berry but it was not a meeting of minds. Sergeant Berry explained that life here had an ebb and flow much like Lough Cuan itself. The people were mainly farmers and fishermen and worked with the seasons be it the grain or potato harvest or the herring season. They were a poor people trying to make ends meet but were always willing to do anyone a good turn – it was a close-knit community.

He urged the new Sergeant to go into some of the houses along the shore where he would see certificates and medals that had been awarded for daring acts of bravery in saving lives from ship wrecks. In such houses he may also see bric-a-brac that could only have come from such wrecks but a small price for a life.

He also urged him to call with some of the widows whose husbands had gone to sea and never returned often leaving them to raise a large family on their own. Only they were never on their own as the community always rallied round and thus each generation grew up with a generosity of spirit that they had witnessed in their own upbringing. Sergeant Berry concluded, that they were a gentle people who didn't need harsh policing, just a reminder now and again that the law should be upheld.

Sergeant O'Neill had not reached the same conclusion. He was in Portaferry for one thing and that was to get out of it as soon as possible and promotion offered the quickest escape route. And promotion wouldn't come from small acts of community policing, but if he could break a smuggling-ring or apprehend those plundering a ship-wreck, then it would reach the Courts and the papers and his superiors would sit up and take notice. With this in mind he had asked for a small patrol boat although he knew nothing about boats or the sea and he had also taken up the defunct post of Receiver of Wreck. There would be no more cosy Sunday nights in Hannigan's. And if he found Hannigan's open on a Sunday night there would be no more Hannigan's.

"Well what are you boys up to at this time of night?" enquired the Sergeant as they pulled alongside the Auld Dog.

"The same as you boys," replied the Captain.

"And what's that?" continued the Sergeant.

"Making a living!" replied the Captain.

Sergeant O'Neill shone his red torch round the Auld Dog, 'as neat as ninepence' as Eddie had remarked and the Sergeant could never tell that it was riding low in the water.

"What's in the kegs?" asked Constable Rogan. Mucker got up and opened one of the kegs, took out a half-gutted dog fish and threw it into the Constable's lap. He nearly jumped out of the boat:

"Watch it Mulligan!" retorted the Constable.

"Ah, ye don't like dog fish," said Mucker, maybe ye'd rather have a wee gilpin and he opened another keg and threw a Gilpin again in the direction of the discomforted Constable.

"Alright, alright, that's enough!" said the Sergeant bringing an end to the altercation as he shone his torch again round the boat.

"What's in that parcel beside you, Bobby?"

enquired the Sergeant. Happy to enter the fray Bobby unwrapped a few sheets of newspaper to reveal his rock-codling:

"They're rock-codling," said Bobby, "Ah get them for the banker. They're his favourite fish, I cud get ye some if ye wud like to try them?"

"We don't like fish," said the Constable dryly.

"Jesus, ye've come to the wrong place then!" laughed Mucker.

"You're right there," muttered the Sergeant inaudibly, "and what else have ye on board, Bobby?"

"Ah, we've plenty more," said Bobby. With a hoard of brandy, tea and tobacco under his feet Mucker shot the Captain a glance from beneath his brow. Bobby opened another keg:

"Look at that Sergeant it's a mackerel. See the way the moonlight plays along its back like a rainbow. Ye could have a couple of those to try if ye like."

"No, that's fine, Bobby," replied the Sergeant. Bobby's intervention and genuine enthusiasm for the catch seemed to convince the Sergeant that this was no more than a fishing expedition.

"The tide will be on the turn, Sergeant, in about ten minutes," said the Captain, "and if ye don't get back up the Lough ye'll be swept over the Bar and on yer way to the Isle of Man. And Ah don't know why anyone would want to go to that God forsaken place," concluded the Captain smiling at Mucker.

With that the Sergeant and Constable got on their way as the Captain let the Auld Dog drift slowly down the Lough knowing that it would be at least another hour before the tide turned. They watched the Sergeant and Constable tie the patrol boat up at the Slip and begin to make their way up Ferry Street towards the police barracks before docking at the Saltpans.

A lantern was burning in the upper room of Hannigan's which was the agreed signal that the coast was clear. Mucker gave two piercing whistles and within minutes dark, shadowy figures could be seen making their way from Hannigan's to the Auld Dog. This line of men started quickly unloading the cargo in a living chain that stretched from the shore to Hannigan's backroom. When the work was completed the backroom was locked and the men sat down to their pipes and pints as if nothing had happened.

"Bobby, we're going into Hannigan's for a wee while, are ye coming?" asked the Captain.

"Nah, I'm going home as my Mammy will be worried about me," said Bobby.

"Fair enough, I'll see ye in the morning, we're at the creels."

"Aye, aye Captain," said Bobby saluting the Captain and hurrying on down the Kilbrae towards home.

"Ah, God bless ye Bobby, home safe from the sea," said his mother sprinkling him with holy water as he came in the door.

"Ah saw yis coming down the Lough. Was that

the Sergeant's boat in front of ye?"

"Aye it was Mammy," said Bobby.

"And what did he want?" continued Martha.

"We were talking about fish and I offered him rock-coding and mackerel but they don't even like fish!"

"Don't like fish! The Lord save us, what kind of folk are they atall" said his mother.

"Eddie was asking about ye and he was singing his Portaferry song."

"Ah, I'm sure he was, he was always a good chanter. I mind the day the teacher got him to sing for the wee curate and he got a sixpence. Didn't he spend it all in the wee shop and gave us all sweets, a kind cratur Eddie. Are ye hungry, Bobby?"

"Aye I'm starving," said Bobby.

"Well, I've a pot of broth made and ye can wash it down with a mug of cold buttermilk."

"The broth's fine but I won't bother with the buttermilk," said Bobby.

"Alright, but the buttermilk's the boy that wud put hairs on yer chest."

"I think my chest is alright – sure who sees it?" said Bobby, as he took his boots off in front of the fire and finished his day with two bowls of hot broth before heading to bed.

7 ANDY

Bobby was up early the next morning and on board the Auld Dog with the Captain and Mucker. Purple streaks of light were beginning to illuminate a grey sky as the dawn was breaking. They would be checking and re-baiting the twenty or so lobster pots that the Captain ran but first stop was Bankmore to unload the rest of yesterday's cargo. Andy McCormick with his pony and trap was waiting for them to arrive. As they neared the shore Mucker jumped from the Auld Dog onto the gravelled beach.

"Well Andy have we kept ye waiting long?" said Mucker.

"Sure I'm up with cock-crow, Mucker, Ah just come down to watch the dawning and have a smoke," replied Andy.

"More like Mrs. Mac kicked ye out of bed again

for snoring," said Mucker.

"You're maybe right Mucker but despite what she says sure I've never heard myself snoring," laughed Andy.

Andy was always cheery and a well-liked character about the town. He had a bushy white beard that was smoke-stained at one side where he constantly smoked his pipe. In the same way that the shoremen made a living from their boats Andy made his from his pony and trap. He would do a bit of rag and bone work, odd jobs for farmers, cart turf, dung and seaweed depending on what turned a shilling. He was also the Captain's delivery man. For this work he would slot a few broad planks across the cart and while it looked as if he had a load of, seaweed or whatever on board, the bottom half of the cart, below the planks, would be filled with tea, tobacco and spirits. This morning the top half of the cart was covered with a tarpaulin which Mucker quickly pulled back.

"Jesus Andy what the hell's that?" shouted Mucker.

"Och it's a dead calf Ah said Ah wud bury it for aul' Shanks."

"For God sake Andy, could ye not just use seaweed or dung as a cover," continued Mucker.

"Well, Ah thought it wud put the new Sergeant off the scent," replied Andy.

"It'll do that alright," said Mucker, "the stink of it wud put anyone off the scent and them boys don't even like dead fish!"

Bobby had already started to unload the Auld Dog handing the various items to Mucker to pack in the bottom of the cart. The Captain had joined Andy for a smoke and a chat. When Mucker was loading the last item below the planks Bobby gave a loud imitation of a cow's call. Mucker thinking the calf was still alive jumped up bumping his head on the planks. When he realised that it was Bobby he caught him in a head-lock.

"Here Andy, when yer burying that calf can ye throw him in as well?" Andy and the Captain had taken a fit of laughing and coughing.

"Hey Mucker, did ye think it was Catherine the Great back to haunt ye?" laughed the Captain, "did Ah ever tell ye, Andy, about Catherine the Great meeting Ivan the Terrible?"

"More than once Captain. More than once!" replied Andy.

With the Captain's story-telling thwarted Andy prepared to get on the road and do his rounds. The Captain's customers included general merchants, well-to-do farmers and landed gentry. None of these considered smuggling a crime, in fact, they thought the Government got enough of their taxes and were more than happy to evade paying any more.

The parish priest also got a cut as the Captain supplied him with wine for the altar and perhaps a bottle of brandy, purely for medicinal purposes, free of charge. He had convinced Father McAleenan with his 'free-trader' argument that what he was doing was not sinful. The Captain now only went to the chapel for weddings and funerals and he saw this act of kindness as his stairway to heaven. He also had a back-up plan as he had made it known that he wished to be buried with a good bottle of brandy. He had concluded that St. Peter and the boys, being fishermen, were 'fond of a drap.' This theory was based on the parable of Jesus turning the water into wine:

"Mind you He didn't just make a few extra bottles of wine," he would say, "there were six stone jars each holding nine gallons of water, now correct me if my sums are wrong, but that's over fifty gallons and that was after they had drank everything in sight!"

If there was any trouble gaining admittance he thought he could sit down with St. Peter with a few glasses of brandy and the matter would be quickly resolved. When voicing this theory, Bobby would always ask if he would have two good legs again when he got to heaven. It caused some debate in Hannigan's, where all such matters of theology were discussed, opinion was divided, between those who thought that you would only have what you went with and those who thought that you couldn't continue to suffer in heaven and, therefore, the leg would be restored. Either way the Captain was happy enough as long as someone remembered the brandy.

"I'll see ye tonight in Hannigan's, Andy" shouted the Captain as they got back on board and watched

Andy make his way back up the loanen to the main road. He cut something of a comic figure with puffs of smoke rising from the front of the cart and a leg of a dead calf dangling out the back.

"Good on ye Andy, good on ye!" shouted Bobby and without looking back he raised his pipe in the air in acknowledgement before disappearing between the hedges.

The streaks of light had now broadened and the morning light was beginning to flood in as the sea-mist dissolved. It was a grey, mild morning with a light wind and a pleasant one to be on the Lough working the creels. Mucker was hauling up the creels and removing any lobsters or crabs and Bobby was re-baiting them and throwing them back overboard. The Captain was pleased with the overall catch as the local hotel would take all the lobster, crab and cod that he could supply. Yesterday's catch of mackerel and gilpin were sorted into fish boxes and these would also be sold to other establishments.

After a tiring day on the Isle of Man trip the creels were a way to relax and they finished up about mid-morning. Bobby took his rock-codling and headed off to have a chat with the banker's wife. He intended going to the Walter Meadow afterwards to listen to the birdsong which was his favourite way to unwind. Mucker was getting on his bike and going out to Marlfield to see if Mary Ellen needed any help and the Captain had some business to talk over with Tommy Hannigan.

8 THE WRECK AT TARA

It had now reached that point of the year where high tides and strong winds were becoming commonplace. Men coming into Hannigan's would stop to warm their hands at the fire and remark:

"Jesus, the nights are away with it now and that wind wud cut ye in two."

A spring tide and strong wind would send waves crashing over the sea wall and against the windows of the fishermen's cottages along the shore front, strewing wrack and sea-weed across the road. As a child Bobby loved sitting by the fire watching the waves crash against the window and he still did. It only reminded his mother of the terrors of the sea and she always said a prayer for any sailors who may be caught out in it.

With the turn in the weather the risks to shipping

navigating the rocky coast-line increased dramatically. Tommy Hannigan was now spending more time in his upper room keeping an eye on all shipping activity coming and going through the Narrows. He knew more than most that fortune favoured the brave and it should be said that a ship foundering on the rocks was not an unwelcome occurrence among the shoremen. It was common for children saying their prayers at night to conclude with:

"God Bless Mammy, God Bless Daddy and may a ship go on before morning."

At this time of year their prayers were often answered. Whilst getting salvage from a ship wreck was fair game there was an unwritten rule that the crew should be saved first. If the crew had been unable to use the lifeboats this duty usually fell to those boats that reached the wreck first. For this reason, although the Captain had been in similar circumstances during his time at sea, he preferred not to be among the first arrivals. Saving a crew took time and effort and often there would be nothing worth salvaging when they returned, as the Captain would say:

"It doesn't put a smoke in yer pipe or a drink in yer glass."

It was the era before the introduction of a local lifeboat service. However, there were two shoremen who generally took on this role without ever taking anything from a wreck other than sailors. They were John McCluskey and Pat Mirren, these were the type of men Sergeant Berry had referred to, and they had accumulated many medals and certificates for their bravery in saving lives over the years. He was, however, wrong to suggest to Sergeant O'Neill that he would see such tokens displayed in their homes, as they were unassuming heroes and such awards were usually thrown to the back of a drawer somewhere.

John was, in fact, a salvage operator and marine diver by trade. If a ship did go down his company had the equipment and expertise to raise it or at least salvage the cargo and this was how he legitimately made a living. He could tell if a ship was going to 'sink or swim' and he would warn approaching shoremen if it was too dangerous to board, although his warnings were not always heeded.

Pat ran a small farm that had its toes in the water at Ballyquintin Point. He was so close to the shore that he could see a ship in distress from the front living room of his farmhouse, or at least, see the flares or hear the horn. He made his living from farming and a bit of herring fishing. Although it was only a short distance from his point on the shoreline to the notorious rocks mid-channel, it still took immense courage to take to a rowing-boat in tempestuous seas but there were many men alive who were glad he did.

The first real stormy night of the year had arrived with a spring tide and it had blown Mucker and the Captain into Hannigan's beside the fire. Updates on the weather conditions were regularly reported by each new arrival until Bobby arrived with the rain running off his oil-skins. Mucker and the Captain could see that he was animated and just about able to contain his excitement:

"There's a brigantine on at Tara Point," said Bobby breathlessly and quietly, "bound for Belfast from Liverpool with a load of stuff on!"

"What about the crew?" asked the Captain.

"John and Pat are already away and I've the Auld Dog ready at the Saltpans," at that Bobby left, and not wishing to draw attention to the situation the Captain and Mucker quietly finished their drinks and followed him out. They were quickly into their oil-skins and away.

While the Lough was rough enough they had seen it much worse but when they turned into the Irish Sea past the Bar they met the full-force of the gale and waves head-on. The Auld Dog seemed to be running up and down hills as the waves peaked and troughed. From there it was a fairly short distance to Tara Point and the brig quickly came into view. The Captain drifted leeside to the brig which offered some protection from the force of the gale. Mucker was quickly on board and lowering crates of whiskey down to Bobby who was loading the sinkers. When he was content with the haul of whiskey Mucker boarded the Auld Dog with a bundle of clothes under his arm.

"What's that ye have Mucker?" asked the Captain as they pulled away from the brig.

"Three suits small, medium and large!"

"And what do ye want them for?" continued the Captain.

"For us three at my wedding," said Mucker.

"The Lord save us, we'll have grown out of them by that time," laughed the Captain as he turned his attention to the serious business of getting home safely. Once over the Bar the storm seemed to be receding as they reached the calmer waters of the Lough. But almost immediately there was a red light fast approaching.

"For feck sake, look who it is," said Mucker.

"Take a bottle of whiskey out of the sinkers and throw it in the bait-bucket," ordered the Captain.

"Quick Bobby get those suits on ye," said Mucker with an urgency that Bobby didn't question and small, medium and large in that order were quickly pulled on and covered over with his oil-skins.

"Bad night Constable," said the Captain calmly.

"Aye and what have you bad boys been up to?" replied the Constable.

"Only good," replied the Captain, "there's a ship on at Tara Point and we went out to see if the crew needed help but John and Pat had already got them aff."

The Constable shone his torch around the boat and the light reflected on the bottle of whiskey in the bait-bucket.

"And what's that?" asked the Constable.

"It was floating in the water near the wreck with a lot of other stuff so we threw it on board," said

Mucker.

"Did ye now?" replied Constable Rogan.

"Aye, what of it?" said Mucker.

Other exchanges, perhaps not all repeatable, followed and culminated in Bobby having to hand over the bottle of whiskey to Constable Rogan.

"Ye'll be hearing more about this," said the Constable as he headed off triumphantly with a single malt and a single bottle. The Captain laughed to himself at the Constable being so pleased with one bottle when he had enough on board to start a pub and Bobby sitting in plain sight with three suits on him.

When they docked at the Saltpans the Captain and Mucker grabbed a few bottles of whiskey each, for drinks on the house, in Hannigan's. With everyone served their whiskey Bobby served up the entertainment doing a strip-tease routine as he divested himself of his oil-skins and three suits.

"Hey Bobby, ye've more skins on ye than an onion!" came a voice from the crowd as Bobby eventually released himself from the final suit, "and don't be taking anything more aff!"

Although not obvious in the darkness of the cargo hold it turned out that they were light blue suits, the like of which had never been seen before among the dark-suited Portaferry men. Mucker was delighted with them:

"By God, we'll be the bobby-dazzlers with them boys on us," said Mucker as he folded them and put them carefully away in Hannigan's backroom. Everyone returned quietly to their whiskey as another uneventful night in Hannigan's came to an end.

But another rather eventful episode which would be remembered and talked about for years to come was about to unfold. Two weeks after the 'Constable and whiskey' confrontation the Captain received a summons to appear before the Portaferry Petty Sessions in the Market House. He was charged with obtaining salvage from a wreck and failing to report it to the Receiver. Meanwhile Bobby had received a subpoena to appear as a prosecution witness. His mother was beside herself:

"What will Ah do Captain if he is imprisoned or sent to Australia?" she implored when the Captain called to explain the situation.

"Martha, if there's anyone going to Australia it's Me as Bobby isn't charged with anything. He only has to give evidence about what happened when we went out to the wreck at Tara... And sure Australia's not that bad," added the Captain, trying unsuccessfully to bring some levity to the conversation.

"What if he says something agin ye, Captain, and ye get into trouble?" continued Martha.

"Well Martha he's never done that before and he'll hardly start now," concluded the Captain with a confidence that Martha didn't fully share.

Mucker had received no notification to attend and it was obvious that the prosecution had targeted

Bobby as the weak-link thinking if there were beans to spill that he would spill them.

9 THE COURT CASE

Martha's rosary beads had been working overtime right up to the morning of the hearing when the Captain called for Bobby. He was looking very smart with his beard and hair neatly trimmed and wearing a white Arran jumper under a navy sailor's jacket. Martha sprinkled them both with holy water as they went out the door and Mucker joined them just up the street. A crowd outside Hannigan's on the Kilbrae voiced their support as they followed them en route to the Market House. Others came out of their houses and joined the throng as they passed. By the time they had reached The Square there were about sixty shoremen and others. Bobby looked around him, not in the least bit nervous, but delighted that he should be at the head of such a band of men, 'I'm the man now Daddy!' he whispered to himself as he entered the Market House. This was the biggest show trial in years, billed as The Captain v The Receiver, and no one wanted to miss it.

The hearing was to take place in the big room upstairs in the Market House. At one end was a raised platform with a desk and two chairs where the Resident Magistrate, Colonel Nugent, and the Clerk to the Court wee Jimmy Hinds sat. To the left of the platform was another desk and three chairs where the Captain, Mucker and Bobby took up their positions. There was a similar arrangement on the right of the platform already occupied by Sergeant O'Neill, Constable Rogan and their legal representative. There was a tension and excitement in the air as the RM commenced proceedings.

RM – Order, order! I ask the Clerk to the Court to read out the charge.

Clerk – This is a case brought by the Receiver of Wreck against Captain Richard Rogers for receiving salvage from a wreck and failing to report it.

RM – Mr. Simmons you are representing the Receiver, is that correct?

Simmons – Yes your Honour.

RM – And Captain Rogers you are representing yourself?

Captain – Yes, with the help of God, yer Honour.

RM – Well, if you've got His help then Mr. Simmons may have a job on his hands [Laughter]. Mr. Simmons you have the floor.

Simmons – Your Honour I call my first witness, Constable Rogan... Constable could you tell the Court about the events on the night of 9th November last.

Constable – It was a bad night and as I was walking at the shore front I noticed a number of boats heading up the Lough. I knew something was up so I got the patrol boat out that was tied up at the Slip. The first boat I met was the Captain's heading back to port. When I checked their boat I found that they had a bottle of whiskey on board.

Simmons – Is this the bottle of whiskey? [holding up the bottle for all to see].

Constable – Yes Mr. Simmons. I was told that they had found it floating near the wreck so I confiscated it.

Simmons - Thank you Constable. Your Honour I call my second witness, Mr. Robert Gibson... Can I begin by confirming that you are Robert Gibson?

Bobby – Yes yer Honour but you can call me Bobby everyone does.

Simmons – Alright Bobby and you can call me Mr. Simmons not yer Honour.

Bobby – Sorry, Mr. Simmons.

Simmons – You don't have to apologise.

Bobby – Oh, sorry. [Laughter]

Simmons – And Bobby when is your birthday?

Bobby – First of January, Mr. Simmons.

Simmons – Which year?

Bobby – Every year! [Laughter]

Captain – [rising] He was born on the first of January 1800, the same day as his father was lost at sea and his poor mother has brought him up on her own all these years.

Simmons – Thank you Captain, I only needed to confirm the date of birth and not a family history. Now Bobby, I see from the papers that you may have a slight disability – does it affect your memory?

Bobby – Yes yer Honour, I mean Mr. Simmons.

Simmons – In what way does it affect you?

Bobby – Ah dunno I forget. [Laughter]

Simmons – Well, can I ask you, Bobby, if your appearance here today is due to you being at the wreck at Tara on 9th November?

Bobby – No Simon, I mean Mr. Simmons, Ah always dress like this with a jacket and gansy. My Mammy knitted me a gansy as it gets very cold out on the Lough. [Laughter]

Simmons – Bobby do you know what would happen to you if you told lies?

Bobby – Yes, I would go to Hell!

Simmons – Is that all?

Bobby – Is that not enough? [Laughter]

Simmons – Bobby, just tell us what happened when you were returning from the wreck.

Bobby – We were stopped by Constable Rogan and he wanted the bottle of whiskey.

Simmons – Is this the bottle of whiskey? [again holding up the bottle]

Bobby – Ah dunno, they all look the same to me and Ah don't even like whiskey, Ah only drink porter. [Laughter]

Simmons – Well what happened next?

Bobby – Mucker and the Constable started to

argue.

Simmons – Mucker, I take it is Mr. Mulligan who is also in Court today. Was he refusing to hand over the bottle?

Bobby – No, he just doesn't like the Constable, he thinks he's smart-assed and lippy. [Laughter]

Simmons – So who handed over the bottle?

Bobby - I did. The Constable said gimme that bottle ye seal and Ah don't know why he said that as I'm not one of the seal people.

Captain – [rising] If I can clarify yer Honour, he said, 'gimme that bottle ye imbecile!'

RM - Is this the sort of language that was used by a member of the constabulary, Mr Simmons?

Simmons – If it was, your Honour, I apologise but I now rest my case as the evidence from both witnesses clearly shows that Captain Rogers obtained salvage from a wreck and failed to report it to the Receiver.

RM – Captain Rogers you have the floor.

Captain – Thank you yer Honour. I would like to draw yer attention to section 50 of the Mercantile Act 1820. [The RM looked to the Clerk of the Court and after rummaging through a bookcase behind the RM wee Jimmy produced the said Act]

RM – Right Captain section 50 you said, I'll read it out for the benefit of the Court – 'Any person who obtains salvage from a wreck and fails within 7 days to report it to the Receiver of Wreck shall be guilty of an offence and liable to a fine or imprisonment' – I'm not sure this is helping your case, Captain.

Captain – Read on yer Honour.

RM – 'And any person who prevents someone from reporting to the Receiver of Wreck will also be guilty of an offence and liable to a fine or imprisonment' – Ah...

Captain – Yes yer Honour I think ye see the legal point. It is my contention that I had 7 days to report the salvage and was prevented from doing so by Constable Rogan confiscating it. [Cheers]

RM – Order please! Mr. Simmons this puts a different complexion on this case it seems that your client may be guilty of an offence and not Captain Rogers.

Simmons – I would suggest your Honour that Constable Rogan was acting as an agent of the Receiver.

RM – And I think you know I would reject that argument. The Constabulary and the Receiver of Wreck are two separate authorities and one cannot act as an agent for the other. Can Constable Rogan please take the stand.

RM – Constable Rogan what would happen if you were found guilty of an offence?

Constable – I would lose my job.

RM – And what would happen if you were sent to prison?

Constable – I don't suppose it would be very pleasant.

RM – I don't suppose it would and what you said

to Bobby wasn't very pleasant either. Can I just say Constable that, that is not how we speak to someone like Bobby in these parts, is that understood?

Constable – Yes your Honour.

RM – I'll tell you what I'm going to do. I'm going to ask you to make a public apology to Bobby and by way of compensation to hand that bottle of whiskey over to him. [Amid loud cheers the Constable meekly complied.]

RM – To conclude I find Captain Rogers 'Not Guilty' and the Receiver to pay costs.

The crowd erupted. Mucker hoisted Bobby, still holding the bottle of whiskey, onto his shoulders and they burst out of the doors into the morning light. His mother was in The Square finishing the last decade of the rosary from the beads in her coat pocket.

"Jesus, Mary and Joseph what has happened?" she exclaimed when she saw Bobby aloft clutching a bottle of whiskey.

"We won Mammy, we won!" shouted Bobby as the crowd carried him down Ferry Street heading for Hannigan's.

Meanwhile the Captain was only starting to make his way out of the hearing room. "That's a free bottle you owe me on next delivery," whispered the RM as he passed the platform. "I'll make it two!" said the Captain smiling. He went over and shook hands with Mr. Simmons:

" Well ye win some and lose some, Mr. Simmons."

"Indeed Captain," said Mr. Simmons quite pale-faced and shocked after being given a lesson in law by an ageing sea Captain.

"It's a bit like fishing," continued the Captain, "sometimes ye think ye have a big fish on and then the line breaks." The Captain walked on hardly needing his crutch as he seemed to be walking on air.

Outside he met Martha and she accompanied him down to Hannigan's. The Captain had told her that Bobby had been 'the star of the show' and with not a little pride she was hurrying home to get some soda bread on the griddle for him. When the Captain flung open the swing-door of Hannigan's, silhouetted as he was in the low winter sunshine, the place erupted again in cheers and applause.

The whiskey was already flowing from remarkably similar bottles to that exhibited in Court. Hannigan had taken the actual exhibit and put it behind the bar as he intended to place it in a display case to mark a momentous occasion. Oul' Ned was already on the fiddle and Bobby was up dancing. The soda bread would have to wait as the party had just begun. The Captain sat down beside Mucker at the fire:

"The Constable knows now ye don't like him very much!" laughed the Captain.

"Ah think he knew that before today," replied Mucker. And so a rather eventful episode came to an end but one that would be long remembered among the Portaferry shoremen.

10 THE GEORGIA

In the aftermath of the Court case the Captain's reputation had soared while the Sergeant's prospects of promotion had plummeted. It had made all the headlines in the newspapers but they were not the headlines that Sergeant O'Neill had been hoping for. In an office somewhere in Belfast, Sergeant O'Neill's superior Chief Inspector Brown, finished his morning coffee, finished reading the paper, leant back in his chair with his feet on the desk, thinking that O'Neill had only made things worse and if he could send him to Siberia – he would!

The first storm of the year and the wreck at Tara had benefited most of the shoremen in one way or another and hopes of a winter where the sea would deliver a bounty on their doorstep were raised. But as time went on their hopes were dashed as the winter turned out to be cold and wet with not enough strong winds to cause much difficulty to shipping. It was a miserable time for the shoremen to be huddled in their boats with the rain dripping off their oil-skins. With freezing hands they hauled up nets and creels often with very little return. The cold seemed to bite into the bone and warm sunny days in the Isle of Man seemed a lifetime away. The re-enactment of the Court case in Hannigan's that had brought great entertainment of an evening was abandoned as men supped silently as they eked out a meagre existence. They were tough times.

Then suddenly, without warning and most unexpectedly their fortunes changed. It was another cold, clear night with the moonlight dancing across the frosted slate roofs. Tommy Hannigan, from his lofty position, could see right into the lantern-lit living rooms of houses in Strangford. There was no sea-mist or wind the folk on each side of the Lough had settled in by the fire for the night. Then the forlorn sound of a ship's horn that seemed to roar down the Lough to Ballyhenry Bay was heard. Hannigan immediately trained his binoculars towards the Narrows and to his surprise found that a huge ship was on the rocks at Killard Point. He checked more than once as a ship that size in difficulty on a clear, calm, moonlit night was something he had never seen before.

It was not long before Bobby appeared and as everyone had heard the horn there was no need for him to tell the Captain the news quietly as he would normally do.

"Wait 'til ye see Captain, wait 'til ye see it," said Bobby almost jumping with excitement, "it's a big Yankie troop ship aground at Bernie's Hole!"

"What about the troops?" asked the Captain.

"Jesus, they're so close to the beach they cud pull their breeks up and paddle ashore. The Strangford lads are already all over it like flies round a cow's arse!"

At that Hannigan's emptied. It seemed that everyone who had a boat of any description were on their way up the Lough. The whole Portaferry fleet, with the Auld Dog leading the way, was mobilised and descending on the wreck. As they neared the ship it was clear that it had broken its back on the rocks. The mournful wailing of the ship's horn, in Bobby's imagination, made it sound like the death throes of a giant whale. In some way it was as the Yankie ship, the Georgia, had found its final resting place and the shoremen were boarding it like vultures to pick it clean.

The Strangford men who had got there first were now organising pony and carts to take away their plunder as quickly as possible. Landing nets had been thrown over the side of the ship to allow the troops to disembark and these now provided the means of access for the Portaferry contingent. Anything that wasn't screwed down would be taken and even some things that had been screwed down were unscrewed and also taken. The haul included wood, furniture, food, ship's gear, carpentry tools, clothes, service uniforms, bicycles, American dollars and so it went on and on.

The Captain knew that the commotion would have alerted Sergeant O'Neill to the drama so he employed wily old mariner, Ned Curran, to act as a decoy. When Ned saw the patrol boat approaching he made it seem as if he was trying to avoid them and the Sergeant gave chase. Ned led the patrol boat into Black Boat Bay which was noted for the long thick sea-weed that grew there. Being unaware of the danger Sergeant O'Neill and Constable Rogan soon found themselves ensnared and had to sit out the night watching the to-ing and fro-ing of the Portaferry boats as they took everything they could get their hands on.

In these situations the Captain rarely boarded a stricken ship as such work was usually left to Mucker. And Mucker was already on board lowering huge consignments of tinned corned-beef down to Bobby. But everything about this wreck puzzled the Captain and so he decided to have a look. Despite having only one leg his upper body strength allowed him to climb the landing nets as well as someone half his age.

The Captain knew his way around a ship and while everyone was in the cargo holds he made his way to the Captain's cabin. There was a desk with three drawers on either side with the top one still locked. The Captain ran his hand along the top of a cupboard and located the key where all Captains seemed to hide it. He quickly opened the drawer and retrieved the ship's log-book and other military papers marked Top Secret. From a quick scan of the papers he knew he had hit the jackpot as he carefully rolled them up and put them in his inside coat pocket. When he returned to the Auld Dog, Mucker and Bobby, had it loaded with a mountain of tinned corned-beef.

"Ah hope ye like corned-beef Bobby," said Mucker.

"Ah've never tasted it before," replied Bobby. That was soon to change as before long he was getting two slices of corned-beef fried with potato bread for breakfast, corned-beef and soda bread sandwiches for lunch and corned-beef with potatoes for dinner.

Whatever the men had got from the wreck they spent the rest of the night concealing it in attics, cubby-holes, burying it in back gardens or under the midden of the outside toilet. The Captain called with Tommy Hannigan and gave him the papers not only to put in his backroom but to put in the safe in the backroom.

"What is it?" asked Tommy.

"It's a pearl oyster, Tommy!" replied the Captain.

The morning dawned as if the night before had never happened. It was crisp and cold but for a change it was dry. The sun was breaking through grey clouds and the slate roofs were running wet. The gloom that had pervaded the shore community for weeks on end seemed to have lifted as quickly as the frost had disappeared from the roof tops. Clusters of men, amid puffs of pipe smoke, gathered at the Slip and the Quay discussing who had got what the night before. Good stories and good humour had returned.

"Hey Bobby, did ye get yer corned-beef yet?" asked one of the old-timers as Mucker and Bobby joined a group of the men.

"Aye, it was good," replied Bobby.

"That's the boy will put hairs on yer chest," continued the old man.

"Well it's better than buttermilk that's for sure!" said Bobby.

It was generally agreed that old Ned Curran had been the hero of the hour. He had literally tied the Sergeant up to allow the shoremen to continue their work unhindered. The Captain had paid him a retainer and others did likewise in recognition of his efforts.. Needless to say he never needed to put his hand in his pocket for a drink in Hannigan's for the next month and more.

While the gloom had lifted from the shore community it had descended on Sergeant O'Neill and Constable Rogan. They had to wait for the high tide in the early hours of the morning before being able to float out of Black Boat Bay. Having spent the whole night helplessly watching the drama unfold in front of them they dejectedly returned to their barracks in the morning, cold and miserable.

In an office somewhere in Belfast, Chief Inspector

Brown, finished reading the morning paper detailing the extensive looting that had taken place when the Georgia ran aground. There was one line that jumped out at him, 'Not A Single Arrest Was Made By The Police.' He got up from his desk to look at the map of the world on the wall behind him just to check where exactly Siberia was.

A week later there was a knock on his office door and his secretary ushered in Bob Johnston from the American Consulate in Belfast. Bob in his smart suit, shiny shoes and rich American accent got straight to the point. He explained that the ship's logbook and secret military documents had been taken from the Georgia and they needed both back to understand why the ship had sank and to avoid military documents falling into the wrong hands. He was brisk about his business, shook hands and concluded:

"Can I ask you Inspector to put your best men on the job?"

"You certainly can Sir and I'll contact them right away."

That afternoon he dictated a letter for his Secretary to send to Sergeant O'Neill detailing the task in hand and intimating that success would probably mean promotion for everyone involved. He needed a breath of air so in the end decided to post the letter himself. As he did so the words, 'Not A Single Arrest Was Made By The Police,' swam around in his head and heavy-hearted at any prospect of success in the endeavor he returned to his office.

Constable Rogan was sorting the post the next morning when he saw the letter from Head Office and immediately handed it to Sergeant O'Neill. The Sergeant looked at it for a moment or two, before hesitantly opening it, half expecting that it was a posting to somewhere worse than Portaferry. Despite being largely incompetent at his job he had an unbounded enthusiasm for it and he saw the order from the Inspector not as an impossible task but an opportunity. He vowed that he would question every man in the town, if need be, to solve the mystery of the missing papers.

A room was set up in the barracks where he and Constable Rogan would conduct their inquisition. The only man they had encountered on the night of the tragedy was Ned Curran and Ned was first to be called in for questioning.

"Now Ned, can you explain why you lured us into Black Boat Bay on the night the Georgia ran aground?" began the Sergeant.

"The only lure I had Sergeant was for pollock they like the sea-weedy places. I thought you were also fishing for them when I saw ye coming into the Bay. Mind you, ye were there long enough to catch a lock of them!"

"We don't like fish!" said the Constable.

And so Ned's interview ended unhelpfully and all the other shoremen who were subsequently questioned continued in much the same vein. They were either not there at all or were innocent onlookers.

The Sergeant considered the crew of the Auld Dog as the prime suspects and the last three interviews of the day were reserved for them.

"Well Mulligan I take it you weren't there on the night of the wreck?" started Constable Rogan.

"Well Rogan happen Ah was," replied Mucker.

"Constable Rogan to you," snapped the Constable.

"And Mr. Mulligan to you, ye remember what the RM told ye about being polite!" Mucker fired back. The Sergeant intervened before they descended into more name calling.

"So, you were there then?" continued the Sergeant.

"Yeah, we went down to have a look at it. Ah don't think there's any law against it although my learned friend, Captain Rogers, could confirm that legal point."

"Did you see any papers relating to the ship?" asked the Sergeant.

"Papers! Jesus, the water was pouring into her, Ah don't think there were any papers that's for sure!" And so Mucker's interview also ran aground and next up was Bobby.

"Well Bobby?"

"Well Sergeant?"

"Mr. Mulligan was telling us that you went down to see the wreck of the Georgia," said the Sergeant, "what did you see?"

"It was like a huge beached whale crying out, stranded on the rocks and couldn't get off. Ah felt sorry for it," said Bobby.

"Only it wasn't a whale Bobby, it was a ship, did you get anything off it?" asked the Constable, who was now getting frustrated with the whole business.

"We didn't get any corned-beef," said Bobby.

"Then why mention corned-beef, Bobby?" continued the Constable.

"Ah dunno, just to tell ye that we didn't get any,' said Bobby. The Sergeant brought this line of questioning to an end as it was heading nowhere.

"Did you see any papers relating to the ship, Bobby?" said the Sergeant getting the questioning back on track.

"Yeah Ah did," said Bobby and the Sergeant and Constable immediately perked up.

"And who had them Bobby?" continued the Sergeant.

"The men in Hannigan's had them spread across the tables looking at them."

"And what sort of papers were they Bobby?" asked the Sergeant trying to conceal his excitement at a potential break-through.

"They were newspapers, the men were reading all about the ship and about some bad boys who took stuff aff it, but it wasn't us," concluded Bobby.

The Sergeant and Constable slumped back in their chairs they should have learned from the Court case that Bobby was 'not that saft.'

The Captain was the last person to be interviewed and he was his usual polite, eloquent and unhelpful self. He did, however, indicate to them how they might wish to proceed:

"Listen Sergeant, we're poor people here finding it hard to make ends meet, particularly, during these winter months. Ah think ye should tell yer American friends that some sort of incentive may be needed for any papers to be released, if someone has them that is."

The Sergeant knew that the Captain knew about the papers and, the Captain knew he knew, but he also knew that he held the trump card and it was now a matter of how much it was worth. He hadn't long to wait for an answer for within two weeks a large envelop arrived at the barracks from Head Office. It contained about a dozen posters offering a reward of £100 for the return of or information leading to the return of the ship's papers. The Sergeant and Constable put them up around the town and left some into Hannigan's and other pubs. Although £100 was a life changing sum of money, even if someone knew that the Captain had the papers, ten times that sum would never induce anyone to tell. As it was, only one man as well as the Captain knew and that was Tommy Hannigan. When the Captain arrived in Hannigan's that evening Tommy handed him the poster and whispered "there's yer pension." The Captain looked at it and replied: "Well, I'm in no hurry to retire just yet, I'm planning another wee run to the Isle of Man now that the weather's picked up.

11 THE ISLE OF MAN

Bobby and Mucker had been hoping that there would be another trip to the Isle of Man before the winter ended. It was always a good day away and it paid better than weeks of freezing work on the Lough. In recent times Mucker was spending a lot of his spare time helping Mary Ellen on the farm as aul' Dan had taken a turn for the worse and was now confined to bed. He found that he was enjoying the farm work more and it was certainly a lot drier than sitting in a boat in the wind and rain.

Meanwhile, Bobby was getting quite a few call-outs with the Gun Club. Since the wreck of the Georgia they were now all kitted out in new khaki jackets and trousers and some had new guns as well – apparently all obtained from an army surplus store in Belfast. With Bobby calling the birds onto the guns they were having considerable success in their hunting expeditions. As a result Bobby and his mother were enjoying a varied diet of duck, pheasant, fish and corned-beef. They may have been poor but they were never going to go hungry.

The appointed day for the Isle of Man trip arrived and Martha was fussing around as usual when a knock came to the door. It was Mucker.

"Yer early Mucker he's still at his breakfast," said Martha.

"Ah just called Martha to tell Bobby I'm not able to go. Ah got word that aul' Dan's a-dying and I'm going to have to go out to Marlfield," said Mucker.

"Och, God help him," said Martha, "tell Mary Ellen that I'll say a wee prayer for him." Mucker could see that Bobby was disappointed that the Isle of Man trip could be cancelled.

"The Captain may still decide to go ahead Bobby," said Mucker, "it's a fair enough day and Steady wud get yis help with the loading."

"Alright Mucker, Ah'll see ye when Ah see ye," said Bobby as he finished his breakfast by the fire.

The Captain had the Auld Dog ready to go when Bobby arrived with the news. He thought about whether they should go or not knowing that it may be late spring before another opportunity arose.

"What do ye think, Bobby?" asked the Captain.

"Mucker said that Steady wud get us help with the loading and it looked to be a fair day."

"Well, he knows," laughed the Captain and at that they drifted off from the quay. Martha was at her usual vantage point, at the shore wall about half-way down the Lough, giving them her blessing of holy water as they passed.

The winter sun was low in the sky and picked up every ripple of water in its light – a diamond sea as the Captain called it. The wind was in their sails and they were making good headway. Mucker was missed as much for his chat and sense of fun as for his physical presence and after a time Bobby and the Captain fell silent and became absorbed in their own thoughts.

The murmuring sound of the water beneath the boat was like a lullaby which the Captain found comforting and reassuring. He thought about what Hannigan had said, that the £100 Reward was his pension, but until that point he had never considered retiring. In fact, he didn't really need the money and he had no one to leave it to either. He had never married, as he thought it would be unfair, as half the time he would be at sea and the other half he would be thinking about going to sea. Still, he had had an adventurous life, won some and lost some (including a leg), and had great stories to tell whenever he got the chance. He didn't need to do the Isle of Man run but it was the trill of it, to be sailing all day, evading the authorities, and getting a nod and a wink from some well-to-do gentlemen about town, signifying that his latest delivery had been well received. Perhaps he should sell the Auld Dog and get a small sailing boat to take part in local regattas and with these and other thoughts they sped on towards their destination.

These quiet moments out at sea was where Bobby felt closest to his father. He could almost feel his presence. If he was looking over his shoulder, as Bobby sometimes thought he was, what was he thinking? Was he proud of him? He must be happy that he sailed with his old friend the Captain. The people at the shore all still had a good word on him. When the Captain spoke about him he sometimes saw a tear come into his eye and he turned away to hide the tears in his own. He thought about his mother praying and worrying at home and the words she still repeated to this day, 'I'll see ye in a couple days he said and I never saw him again and he never saw you.' She always said her prayers and was always first at the chapel and still that happened, he didn't understand God. He didn't understand many other things as well but he always tried to be the 'the man of the house' for his mother's sake.

Mucker was always good at distracting Bobby from such maudlin thoughts but his absence today allowed him to indulge more than usual and to such an extent, that in an instant, the Isle of Man seemed to magically appear in front of him. Within a short time he could see Eddie on the wooden jetty and his mood lifted immediately.

"Alright Steady," shouted Bobby, throwing Eddie the ropes as they approached the jetty.

"All good Bobby, where's yer big mate Mucker did ye throw him overboard?"

"Nah, aul' Dan's a-dying so he had to stay at home with Mary Ellen."

"I'm sorry to hear that," said Eddie, "what about yer mother?"

"She's grand, she was talking about ye singing at school and buying sweets in the wee shop beside the chapel," said Bobby.

"She's a great memory, Bobby, 'cos that wasn't yesterday. And how's you Captain?" asked Eddie as the Captain climbed stiffly out onto the jetty.

"Grand Steadward, only Ah keeping getting pains in my left leg," said the Captain.

"But sure ye haven't got a left leg," said Eddie.

"Ye don't have to tell me that Steadward but somehow Ah feel pain in it at times, maybe it's just old age," said the Captain.

"Hey Thomas, could ye give us a wee hand later?" shouted Eddie to a young man mending fishing nets further along the beach and he got a thumbs up in response.

"He's a good lad, Thomas, he'll help Bobby with the loading," said Eddie, as the three of them made their way to the hut and Eddie got the kettle on the boil.

"Well did yis get anything aff that big Yankie ship that went down?" asked Eddie as he poured the tea.

"Sure didn't aul' Ned tie the Sergeant and his mate up in Black Boat Bay and we got whatever we wanted. Bobby's been eating corned-beef ever since!

"Did ye bring any with ye Bobby Ah love the

corned-beef?" said Eddie.

"Only in my soda bread,' replied Bobby.

"Here give us a wee nip of it to taste," said Eddie, "by God that's good stuff, wud ye bring us a tin of it out, the next time yer over," said Eddie savouring the morsel of beef in his mouth.

"I'll bring ye more than one," said Bobby, "I'm fed up eating it for breakfast, dinner and tea!"

"Do ye know what happened it Captain?" continued Eddie, "it was so clear that night I cud nearly have walked over to yis."

"That's what the Yanks are trying to find out," said the Captain, "and they've offered a £100 Reward for anyone who can produce the ship's papers."

"That's powerful money Captain," said Eddie.

"Aye, but when ye get to our age sure money's not everything, good friends, good times, good memories and enough to get by is all ye need."

"Never a truer word, Captain, never a truer word," concluded Eddie.

At that Thomas called in to give Bobby a hand with the loading. The Captain and Eddie lit their pipes and reminisced about some of those old times and memories.

After a time Bobby and Thomas returned having completed their task and the Captain slipped Thomas a couple of shillings. As Thomas made his way back to his nets Bobby and the Captain took their leave of Eddie.

"We've an hour or more Steadward 'til the tide

turns so we're going to see if there's any arm-wrestlers in that tavern ye mentioned," said the Captain.

"Fair enough, if the weather changes ye know where I am and ye can stay the night," said Eddie, "tell yer mother Ah was asking for her Bobby and tell Mucker Ah was sorry to hear about aul' Dan."

"Will do Steady," replied Bobby.

The Captain and Bobby made their way up a dusty street leading away from the shore. There were creels, nets and buoys outside many of the houses that they passed and old men who seemed also to have been set outside until their wives got on with the housework.

Eventually they arrived at the tavern which was a white-washed, thatched cottage. Inside it was dimly lit with a stale smell of beer and tobacco. The Captain ordered two bottles of porter and sat down at a table close to other drinkers. The arm-wrestling routine had been well rehearsed by Bobby and the Captain over the years. The Captain challenged Bobby to an arm-wrestling match for the stake of a tanner speaking loudly enough for the men at the next table to hear and to take an interest. It always played out the same, Bobby who was obviously of a slighter build than the Captain appeared to be winning until somehow the Captain turned the tables at the last moment.

This caught the attention of the men watching on and allowed them to think if Bobby could nearly beat the Captain then they definitely could:

"I'll raise ye 'til a shilling," said one of the men. The Captain put down two tanners and put down his challenger just as easily. Eddie was right these were gambling men and soon the whole bar was involved with stakes being raised each time. The coins were piling up on the table when the whisper went round - 'Get Big Billy.' Within about five minutes Big Billy and his mate arrived in the tavern. He was just as muscular as Mucker but taller.

"What about double or quits Captain to give the lads a chance to win their money back?" said Big Billy.

It was obvious that Billy was the local strong man and something of a local hero as the men in the tavern nodded and smiled at one another at the prospect of the Captain about to meet his match. The Captain was totally unfazed as he had taken down bigger men than Billy in his time.

"Ah dunno," said the Captain, "double stakes would take it to nearly a fiver and Ah don't want to take any more money aff ye."

"Ah don't think ye wud be," said Big Billy confidently and the men laughed at the very idea of the Captain beating their champion. At that Billy rolled up his sleeve and sat down opposite the Captain. They locked hands and the men gathered round roaring their support.

There was no noticeable movement from either side. Whilst the Captain had powerful upper body strength it was his vice-like grip that was the key. His technique was to grip an opponent's hand so firmly that it stopped the circulation of blood to the fingers which would then turn purple. At that point an opponent's eyes would start to water and this was always the signal for the Captain to make good his advantage. It played out as it always had done. Big Billy couldn't feel his hand at all and when the Captain launched his attack he had no response as the Captain banged his hand down on the table. It was a lone voice that cried out:

"Good on ye Captain, good on ye!"

The atmosphere seemed to have been sucked out of the tavern and Big Billy, humiliated on his own turf, retreated to the bar and ordered a whiskey. Bobby gathered up the coins into both pockets of his jacket, they finished their drinks and got up to leave. They found the door blocked by Billy and his mate.

"Ye didn't think we wud just let ye walk out with all our money now, did ye?" said Big Billy grinning. Almost before he had finished his sentence the Captain delivered a blow to the side of his face with his crutch. Billy went down and he wasn't getting up. His mate came forward and the Captain caught him by the throat and almost throttled the life out of him before throwing him to the floor. He wasn't getting up either or if he was wise he wasn't. All the time Bobby was behind the Captain throwing wild punches in mid-air.

"Maybe see yis again sometime," said the Captain tipping his cap to the rest of the bar. Outside Bobby was still throwing punches.

"Ye should have let me hit him, Captain, ye should have let me hit him!" repeated Bobby excitedly.

"Sure Bobby if you had hit him with one of those ye wud have knocked him into next week," said the Captain.

"Aye, ye're right there Captain, ye're right there!" said Bobby. The Captain looked up at the gathering clouds:

"Ah think the weather's changing Bobby, if Mucker was here we'd maybe go to Steadward's but Ah don't want to bring any trouble to his door, we need to get going." Bobby was still running on adrenaline when they reached the jetty. The Captain got on board as Bobby loosened the ropes, stepped easily onto the bow and they were away.

"Ye can keep the money Bobby as yer due double wages today with Mucker not being here," said the Captain as he tacked the Auld Dog into the wind.

"Jesus Captain, my Mammy will think Ah've robbed the bank when she sees all those coins," said Bobby, jingling the coins in both pockets and relishing the prospect of slapping them down on the kitchen table.

12 THE AULD DOG LIMPS HOME

The Captain was right about the changing weather, as thunder could be heard rumbling somewhere in the distance or in the high heavens. Bobby was afraid of thunder, as he thought it was God being angry, but as he was still fighting imaginary opponents he never took it under his notice. If there was going to be a thunder storm the Captain was hoping that the stiff breeze would keep them ahead of it.

It was a cloudy, moonless night and the Auld Dog was a black boat, in a black night, sailing effortlessly and invisibly to port. As they surged past the Rocking Goose the lights of Portaferry came into view and the Captain triumphantly exclaimed, "Home Sweet Home, Bobby!"

The words were still on the breeze when suddenly there was a massive impact to the stern. The Captain heard the cargo shift and knew immediately that the Auld Dog was about to capsize. Bobby and the Captain were thrown into the freezing water with the sinker kegs around them plunging to the bottom. The false stern of the Auld Dog had broken off and floated like a wooden box. The Captain grabbed it and stabilised it by putting his crutch across its length. He then caught hold of Bobby who frantically grabbed one end of the crutch. Suddenly they realised that there was someone else thrashing around in the water beside them and from the screams they knew it was Sergeant O'Neill. The Captain grabbed him and he caught the other end of the crutch.

"Where's the Constable?" shouted the Captain.

It was unclear what the Sergeant was saying but clear enough that he was on his own. The upturned carcass of the Auld Dog floated on and they found themselves spinning round and round in the notorious Routen Wheel at the Bar with the possibility of being sucked under at any moment. The Captain kept a calm head while those on either side of him were losing theirs.

"Can ye swim Sergeant?" shouted the Captain.

"Aye," replied a voice in the darkness.

"When Ah tell ye to let go swim for Killard and the tide will land ye on the beach."

The Captain gave the signal and the Sergeant disappeared splashing into the darkness. He knew that Bobby could swim, after what had happened to his father, his mother had insisted on him learning. As a boy she had taken him out to Ballyhenry Bay until she was satisfied that he could swim well enough to save himself if he ever fell overboard. And while he could easily swim back to a boat this was a more serious situation – there was no boat!

"Bobby, listen to me," shouted the Captain, "when ye get back tell Tommy to hand in the papers and to get the Reward for you and yer mother, do ye hear me?"

"Ah do Captain,"

"Now, are ye ready Bobby?" shouted the Captain.

"What about you, Captain?" replied Bobby.

"Sure I can't swim and if Ah cud sure with one leg I'd keep going round and round."

The Captain was using black humour to try and minimise the seriousness of the situation as he knew if Bobby started to panic he would be gone. Most of the old-timers at the shore couldn't swim, they held the view that being able to swim only prolonged the inevitable and the sea was entitled to its catch from time to time.

"Right Bobby the tide's with ye – Go!" and at that Bobby too disappeared into the darkness.

Bobby was a fairly good swimmer but was struggling to make headway. The water was surging in his ears and screaming through his head. He tried a few strong strokes but kept going under. Then he heard a voice as clear as if someone was whispering in his ear:

"The coins, Bobby, the coins!"

It wasn't the Captain's voice and he didn't know what it meant as he was once again going under. It was only when the voice came a second time and repeated:

"The coins, Bobby, the coins!" that he realised the coins in his coat pockets were weighing him down.

He struggled out of his jacket which sank to the bottom and he bobbed up to the surface. He was gulping air and water almost in equal measure but at last he was making some headway. He thought about his mother at home praying and worrying and it somehow gave him strength. By this stage he was exhausted and the tide was assisting his progress more so than his swimming. He could feel the kelp beds clawing at his legs trying to entangle him and pull him down to the depths. Exhausted and with not an ounce of strength left he was washed up on Killard beach unable to move and seemingly lifeless.

The first streaks of light were beginning to break in the dark morning sky and the first smoke was beginning to rise from the chimneys of the fishermen's cottages just above Killard beach. One fisherman emerged to take his readings of the tide and weather and walked down to the beach. He saw what he thought were two seals but on closer inspection discovered Bobby and the Sergeant within about one hundred yards of one another. They looked more dead than alive but nonetheless alive. He roused a few of the other fishermen and carried them into two adjoining cottages. They had no idea where they had come from or who they were. The womenfolk were well used to dealing with such situations and they were left in their capable hands as the men readied their boats and nets for a day's fishing.

They were immediately helped out of their wet clothes and put straight to bed. Bobby was delirious, he thought the wooden rafters of the bedroom ceiling was the hull of a boat that he was under. The weight of the bedclothes was like the sea pressing down on him and he tried to kick them off, he was trying to swim but couldn't move his arms. In the brief moments when he came to he was crying out for the Captain and his Mammy. The Sergeant was in the cottage next door similarly suffering from exhaustion and shock and barely able to move.

The same streaks of morning light were now breaking on the opposite side of the Lough. Martha had heard the thunder the night before and assumed that the Captain had decided to stay put in the Isle of Man. But it didn't stop her worrying. The rain that the thunder had threatened had just started to arrive and she threw an old oil-skin of Bobby's across her shoulders with the hood up as she went to the shore wall to check for their arrival.

The scene that confronted her almost took her breath away. The Auld Dog had limped home and lay upturned near the Saltpans. She let out a wail that was almost inhuman and seemed to come from her very soul. On hearing it, wee Mrs. Watterson who was getting Wullie's breakfast ready, ran out to the door. She saw a figure slumped by the wall and immediately ran to its assistance.

"The Lord save us Martha it's you, in the name of God, what's happened?" she cried. Martha pointed towards the Auld Dog: "Not Bobby! Not Bobby!" she sobbed. Wullie who had heard the commotion hurried out and they both helped Martha to her own fireside.

"I'll get her a wee hot whiskey to calm her nerves," said Wullie. He met a boy wheeling a bicycle just outside the door and slipped him a penny.

"Here son will ye cycle out to Marlfield and get Mucker. Tell him to get here as quick as he can."

The boy determined to earn his penny jumped on the bike and was up over the Kilbrae as if his life depended on it. In a short time the familiar figure of Mucker, hunched over the handlebars of his bike, with his coat-tails flying in the wind, came over the Kilbrae. The boy who had started off from Marlfield at the same time was now more than half a mile behind.

Wullie quickly explained what had happened and pointed to the Auld Dog stranded at the Saltpans. Mucker was quickly across the beach and secured its ropes. He checked underneath the boat to ensure that no one had been trapped but it was empty. He made his way back to Bobby's house with Wullie. The hot whiskey had settled Martha and she had been put to bed. Mucker went into the room but she didn't open her eyes. Her lips were moving in constant prayer and every now and then she whispered, "Lord have mercy on us. Not Bobby, not my Bobby!"

Mucker didn't speak he came out of the room, sat down by the fire, put his face in his hands and wept. Aul' Dan had died overnight and this morning he was faced with losing the two best friends anyone could ever have. He blamed himself for everything. Although aul' Dan had made his peace with Mucker on his death-bed and conceded that he had been a stubborn old man, he still blamed himself for putting Mary Ellen's life on hold for the past twenty years. On reflection he thought he should have told Bobby to tell the Captain to put the Isle of Man trip off. If he had been there he may have persuaded the Captain to stay overnight in the Isle of Man or he may have taken more care in positioning the load and prevented the Auld Dog from capsizing. With these and other such thoughts running through his head he heard Wullie approaching the fire:

"What am Ah going do, Wullie, what am Ah going to do?" he almost pleaded.

"I'll tell ye what yer going to do," said Wullie, "yer going to get the men out and check every island and beach up and down the Lough. Ye know the Captain, sure Bobby and him are probably sitting there somewhere waiting for yis!"

Wullie was old enough to have seen many such sea tragedies play out before and the folk on dry land, who had no part in it, always blamed themselves for something they should have done or had not done. He recalled as a boy watching an old fishing boat capsize at Oldcourt just off Strangford with two brothers on board. Their mother watched their fate from the shore and immediately blamed herself for not stopping them going out in bad weather. His mother and father gave her what comfort they could in much the same way as he and Winnie had tended to Martha. In short, Wullie knew it was better working through these things rather than lying under them. Having something to do, no matter how improbable or impracticable, was much preferable. This immediately raised hope in Mucker and he was off rousing the men for a search of the Lough. At the Slip he met Constable Rogan coming down Ferry Street in a rather distressed state:

"Hey Mucker, the Sergeant went out in the patrol boat last night and hasn't returned. I told him not to go as the red light on the patrol boat wasn't working properly."

Mucker explained that the Captain and Bobby were also missing and invited him to join him in the punt to help with the search. Like Mucker, the Constable was glad to be doing something useful but it was a most unlikely alliance to see Mucker and the Constable sitting side by side as they rowed up the Lough.

Mucker was co-ordinating the search and directing the men to the most likely and unlikely spots where they could have been washed up. By mid-afternoon they had checked every possible location from the Bar Mouth to the Dorn at Ardkeen but without success. They had picked up some wreckage from the patrol boat and it was obvious what had happened. The Captain hadn't seen the patrol boat without its red light and the Auld Dog in the black night would have been invisible to the Sergeant. As a result they had collided with the patrol boat coming off the worse. The search was called off and, lost in their own thoughts, Mucker and the Constable rowed silently towards the shore until eventually the Constable spoke:

"You know Mucker, the Sergeant wasn't just my best friend, he was my only friend here."

"And ye know Constable," replied Mucker, "if he had been the only one missing we would still be out looking for him."

They parted at the Slip perhaps now understanding each other slightly better. Mucker thought about the Constable going back to the cold, dark barracks alone and while he had lost two dear friends the whole shore community were his people and his friends. The Constable now also understood that old Sergeant Berry was right, that these people would do anyone a good turn, and may even risk their own lives in doing so.

Winnie knew immediately by the look on Mucker's face that the search had been unsuccessful. They both knew that if lost sea-men were not found within twenty-four hours that they would now only be looking for bodies rather than survivors.

"Here Mucker sit down and have a boul of broth and there's some wheaten bread there that ye like," said Winnie avoiding the obvious questions and trying to put a brave face on it.

"How's Martha?" asked Mucker.

"Ah can't get her to take a bite. She's only had a few sips of water as her lips are parched with the praying. I'm worried about her Mucker," said Winnie unable to conceal her anguish.

"Jesus, if there's a God in Heaven atall he'll spare her," said Mucker almost angrily as he finished his broth, "Ah'll have to get going and get tidied up to give Mary Ellen a hand at the wake."

"Sure try and get a wee rest before going out to Marlfield, Mucker, ye've been on the go since yesterday morning," said Winnie who had mothered and fussed round Mucker since he was a small boy and she still did.

"I'll try," said Mucker knowing full well that with so much going on that it would be impossible to sleep.

13 HOME FROM THE SEA

Meanwhile on the other side of the Lough Bobby was drifting in and out of sleep. He knew now that he was in a strange bedroom and not under a boat. Also, that there was a woman attending to him and it was not his mother. She was spooning him fish-soup, that tasted like salt water and made him sick, which seemed to please her as she said it was 'flushing him out.'

By the next morning Bobby was brightening and discovered that he was in Mr. and Mrs. Swail's cottage at Killard.

"Yer friend's next dure!" said Mrs. Swail as she brought him more fish-soup.

"The Captain?" said Bobby, raising his head from the pillow.

"No, I think he said he was a Sergeant." Bobby slumped back on his pillow and for the first time the memory of the incident came flooding back to him.

He bit his lip as he tended to do when he was upset and fighting back tears he lay looking up at the rafters.

The Sergeant, who was in Mr. and Mrs. McDonald's cottage next door, was recovering slightly quicker than Bobby. Although still weak he was able to visit Bobby and sat with him for most of the afternoon.

"The Captain saved our lives, Bobby," he said.

"Ah know," said Bobby sadly, "and someone else helped me as well."

"Who was that?" asked the Sergeant.

"Ah dunno," said Bobby, as he drifted back into sleep and the Sergeant just thought he was rambling and disorientated.

On the third morning Bobby was able to take his first faltering steps and he became consumed with thoughts of his mother. He told the Sergeant that he had to get home straight away as his Mammy would be worried about him. He was becoming increasingly agitated and upset. Mrs. Swail suggested that when her husband came home from the fishing that evening that he would row them across but for now he should rest and save his strength. The thought of imminently getting home had a calming effect on Bobby and he fell into a deep sleep.

He slept right through until early evening when he was awakened by the sound of men's voices and the smell of tobacco smoke and for a moment he thought he was back in Hannigan's, until he realised that Mrs.

Swail was sitting by his bedside:

"Wud ye take another wee drap o' soup, Bobby, before ye go?" she asked. Bobby politely declined wondering to himself why everything that was supposed to be good for you tasted as if it would be bad for you.

On hearing the voices Mr. Swail and the Sergeant, who had been talking, came into the room and helped to get Bobby ready. Mr. and Mrs. McDonald came in to see them off as the Sergeant took Bobby's arm and helped him down the beach to a big old rowing boat that had been in the Swail family for generations. The tide was with them and they drifted gently down to Strangford and across to the Slip at Portaferry. The Sergeant got out first and then helped Bobby out of the boat. They thanked Mr. Swail for his kindness and he was away back up the Lough as the darkness began to creep in.

Winnie and Wullie were sitting by the fire when they heard the latch lifting as Bobby and the Sergeant walked in:

"Jesus, Mary and Joseph is it yerself Bobby?" said Winnie, blessing herself and jumping up to embrace him.

"Aye, it is Winnie, where's Mammy?"

The Sergeant sat down beside Wullie to tell him what had happened as Winnie bundled Bobby in to see his mother.

"Martha, Martha it's Bobby!"

Martha weakly opened her eyes and couldn't

believe it was Bobby standing in front of her. She reached out to take his hand to ensure that she wasn't dreaming or that it wasn't an apparition before her. Bobby was shocked at the state of his mother. Her face was as grey as a heron's wing and her eyes were glazed and darkened. Bobby threw his arms around her neck:

"Don't leave me Mammy, don't leave me!" he cried, and Winnie buried her face in her apron being almost overcome with the emotion.

"Yer foundered, Bobby, get up to the fire for I'm alright now!" said Martha in a hoarse whisper.

Sergeant O'Neill was getting up to leave when they came back into the room and despite Winnie trying to get him to stay for something to eat he decided to go on. Wullie followed him out and called into Mucker's. He had buried aul' Dan earlier that day and having barely slept for three of four days he had crashed out on his big leather chair by the fire. The house felt cold and damp as the fire hadn't been lit during that time. He was startled when Wullie shook him by the shoulder excitedly imploring him to:

"Come quickly, Mucker, come quick!"

Mucker hardly knew where he was but on seeing Wullie he immediately thought that something had happened to Martha, he could hardly take anymore, but regardless he dashed out after Wullie. On entering Martha's and seeing Bobby sitting by the fire, he was speechless, he swept him up in a massive bear-hug that lifted him off his feet.

"Jesus Bobby, Ah didn't think I'd ever see ye again!" said Mucker unable to hold back the tears running down his face. "And what about the Captain?"

Bobby just shook his head and Mucker knew this was not the time to pursue that question. Winnie got the kettle on as Mucker sat looking at Bobby as if a miracle had happened before his eyes. Wullie grabbed his coat and said he was going up to Hannigan's with the news. On his way home the Sergeant had also passed Hannigan's and he could hear voices from within. He had thought about going in to tell them what had happened, but was afraid that he would be blamed for the tragedy, so he trudged on unnoticed through the dark streets back to the barracks.

The return of Bobby was like a ray of sunshine breaking through a winter sky. It lifted everyone's mood, not least, his mother's. If Bobby needed nursing back to health there was only one woman for that job. Within a couple of days she was back on her feet and Winnie had returned to her own hearth and home. There was a constant stream of people calling to see Bobby and to hear his account of what had happened. The most intriguing part of the story was the mysterious voice warning Bobby about the coins. Bessy Murray was the first to put forward the theory that it was Martha's prayers being answered by Bobby's Guardian Angel. The parish priest concurred that this could very well be the case and the theory gained support among the devout chapel-goers. Despite being a member of that group, Martha's view and that of the majority of the shore community, was that it was the voice of his father who was not prepared to let the sea claim Bobby as another victim.

The kettle was never off the stove as Martha welcomed everyone who called. The Chairman of the Gun Club left in a brace of birds. Martha hung one up in the outside shed until she was able to prepare it and left one next door for Winnie. The banker and his wife called, very nice, well-spoken, well-mannered people thought Martha and it was obvious that they held Bobby in high regard.

"I hope you'll soon be dropping us in a few wee rock-codling, Bobby, when you get up and about again," said the banker on leaving.

"Ah hope so too," replied Bobby, as his mother showed them to the door.

Tommy Hannigan came in with some bottles of porter for Bobby and a bottle of port for Martha with the advice that a wee glass at night would help her get off to sleep. On seeing Tommy, Bobby immediately remembered what the Captain had said about the papers and the Reward.

"Are ye sure that's what he said, Bobby?" asked Tommy.

"They were his exact words and nearly his last words to me, Tommy," said Bobby sadly remembering the moment.

Tommy wasted no time, he went straight back to the pub and retrieved the papers from the safe in the backroom. His knock on the barrack's door was answered by Constable Rogan who showed him into a room with Sergeant O'Neill. Tommy produced the papers and told them that Martha and Bobby were to receive the Reward. The Sergeant looked at the papers amazed that they were now actually in his possession but he asked no questions as he may have a done a short time ago. He was beginning to understand the ebb and flow of the shore community, it was immaterial how the papers came into Tommy's possession, things seemed to work better when there was least said. The Sergeant thanked Tommy and said that he would deal with it immediately.

The next morning saw the Sergeant and Constable on the first mail coach out of Portaferry for Belfast. They considered the papers of such importance that they had decided to deliver them personally to the Chief Inspector. It was late morning by the time they arrived at the Chief Inspector's office. He was puzzling over the last clue of the crossword in the morning paper: 'circus entertainers six letters' when his secretary announced the arrival of Sergeant O'Neill and Constable Rogan. 'Ah, Clowns!' he said, as he finished the crossword and folded the paper.

It was perhaps an understatement to say that the Chief did not hold his two junior officers in the highest regard. They had lost a high profile Court case which set an unhelpful precedent as regards salvage, the Georgia had been completely looted and they hadn't made a single arrest and recently they had smashed up the patrol boat. The Chief Inspector hid his misgivings and greeted them warmly.

"Well, what has brought you all the way to the Big Smoke from the back-end of the Ardes?" he asked cordially, shaking hands with both of them.

When Sergeant O'Neill produced the papers from the Georgia he almost fell off his chair in disbelief. He spread the papers out on the desk thinking that there must be some mistake, but no, they were undoubtedly the ship's log and other military papers from the Georgia. He hastily wrote a note for his secretary to take across town to Bob Johnston in the American Consulate. While waiting for Bob Johnston, the Sergeant told the Chief Inspector all about the sea tragedy and how he owed his life to the Captain, who was now lost at sea. The Chief Inspector was beginning to think, that he was perhaps a bit harsh about his Siberian idea, when Bob Johnston's voice was heard in the corridor.

Bob Johnston in a long winter coat and fedora trilby was shown into the office. On being introduced by the Chief he shook hands vigorously with Sergeant O'Neill and Constable Rogan.

"Well, have you good news for me?" asked Bob in his rich American twang. The papers were still spread out on the desk. Bob studied them intently and was absolutely delighted:

"Yep, that's them, that's what we were looking

for!" he concluded. He shook hands again with everyone as he carefully folded the papers and placed them in the inside pocket of his overcoat.

"I take it that you can get the Reward delivered?" said Bob as he paid out £100 in bank notes onto the desk, "and I take it that the Constabulary will reward your intrepid investigators, Chief?"

"Indeed we will," replied the Chief Inspector. Sergeant O'Neill and Constable Rogan had never been referred to as 'intrepid investigators' before, they were not exactly sure what it meant but they were sure that the whiff of promotion was in the air. After saying their good-byes to Bob Johnston, the Chief took the Sergeant and Constable out for lunch before they embarked on their long journey back.

When he had seen them off and had returned to the office, he was still pinching himself in disbelief, he too would be in line for promotion for cracking such an important case. He really couldn't believe what had just happened so he called his secretary into the office:

"Maria, wasn't Sergeant O'Neill, Constable Rogan and Bob Johnston here today?"

"Yes Chief."

"That's alright, I was just checking!" and Maria left even more puzzled than the Chief Inspector.

It was late that evening by the time the Sergeant and Constable returned to Portaferry but they were up early the next morning to deliver the good news and Reward to Martha. On passing Mucker's house the Constable said that he would call in to tell Mucker the news. From the most unlikely beginnings these two had somehow reached a mutual understanding and could now be said to be on friendly terms. The Sergeant went on to Martha's and was pleased to see Bobby looking hale and hearty. He felt a special bond with Bobby as they both shared a near death experience and knew what it was like to fight to their last breath.

"Well Martha we were up in Belfast yesterday and the man from the American Consulate, true to his word, paid out the Reward and no questions asked," said the Sergeant as he counted out £100 on the kitchen table. Bobby was rather disappointed at what £100 in notes looked like. He was expecting a treasure chest filled with gold and silver coins. His mother folded the notes and put them in the tea caddy on the mantle-piece.

"I don't think you should keep all that money sitting around, Martha," advised the Sergeant, "you should get it into the Bank."

"Ah'll do that Sergeant the next time the banker and his wife call to see Bobby," said Martha. Bobby couldn't quite believe the next transformation of the £100 pounds into a small blue bank book with numbers scribbled inside. In fact, he didn't care for the money at all, no matter what it looked like, he would gladly throw it all into the Lough without a thought if it would bring the Captain back.

14 MUCKER'S BIG IDEA

Although Bobby had recovered physically from his ordeal he was totally grief-stricken about the loss of the Captain. He never went into Hannigan's anymore as he could not bear to see Mucker sitting by himself at the fire or someone else sitting in the Captain's chair.

Each morning before breakfast he would go out to look up and down the Lough and along the beach. After breakfast he would get a punt out and scan beaches and islands around the Lough. He would then return and sit up in the Walter Meadow aimlessly watching the Lough flow past. For Bobby the birds had stopped singing or talking to him.

His mother knew exactly how he felt as the Captain had been like a father to him. She tried to reassure him by telling him that they would get a memorial erected for the Captain in the graveyard and that he would probably now be sitting in Heaven talking to his father. Bobby was not so sure as the Captain always wanted to be buried with a bottle of brandy, to assist in his admission to Heaven, and his wish had not been granted.

Mucker, who had grown up with Bobby, and knew him almost as well as his mother had tried and failed to divert Bobby's train of thought on to a brighter outlook. He had suggested that they should try to locate his jacket with all the coins in it or some of the sinkers that had went down that night. And while there would be little prospect of success, this would normally have been a day's fun messing about on the Lough, but Bobby was totally disinterested. Then Mucker had an idea but he would have to talk to Mary Ellen about it.

Mucker's big idea was to bring forward the wedding and get Bobby, as best man, involved in all the arrangements but he was unsure if Mary Ellen would agree, as after all, she had just buried her father.

"Well they can hardly say we're rushing into it now, Mucker," said Mary Ellen, when Mucker made the suggestion and she was only too glad to do something that could help Bobby.

That evening they called with Martha and Bobby to announce their plans and for a fitting of the light blue suits that Mucker had got off the wreck at Tara.

When Bobby went to his room to try on the suit Martha made it clear to Mucker and Mary Ellen that she would be using the 'Captain's money,' as she called it, to pay for the wedding and reception. Most wedding receptions in the town amounted to 'a bit of a do' in one of the local pubs but Martha was insistent that it would be held in the Nugent Arms, the best hotel in town, and that there would be no restrictions on the numbers. She cut any arguments short by simply stating that it was what the Captain would have wanted.

When Bobby emerged from his room Mary Ellen was more than pleased:

"By God Bobby, ye look a million dollars, I don't know what I'm doing marrying Mucker!" she laughed.

"Here Bobby, go next dure to Winnie, she's got a full length mirror on her wardrobe dure and ye can see for yerself," said Martha. When he was gone Mucker got changed into his suit and Bobby returned with Winnie in tow.

"God save us Martha, Ah was wondering who was coming in on me. Ah thought it was yer man from the American Consulate before Ah recognised Bobby. Mind you, the trousers might need taking up a wee bit," said Winnie, before turning her expert eye to Mucker as she looked him up and down.

"The length's perfect on you Mucker but it's a bit tight at the waist. Ah'll let the trousers out an inch or so for ye," said Winnie.

"Maybe about a foot or so Winnie," said Bobby,

and everyone laughed as it was the first time that Bobby's sense of humour had surfaced since the boating incident.

"Do ye mind the night we got the suits Bobby?" said Mucker, "you were sitting in the stern with three suits and oil-skins on ye and a bottle of whiskey at yer feet. The Constable was going mad for the whiskey not knowing that we had enough on board to start a pub. Ah'll maybe tell him that when he's leaving, he might see the funny side of it now!"

"And maybe he won't," said Bobby, "and ye'll end up in the clink with Mary Ellen waiting another twenty years!"

"Well that's an idea, Bobby," laughed Mary Ellen.

Mucker had deliberately retold the story to give Bobby the sense that the times they had with the Captain should be fondly remembered rather than mourned as they were indeed the best of times.

"We're going up to Lawson's tomorrow Bobby, shirts, ties and shoes and that's you two sorted. You'll be easily fitted Bobby but we'll probably have to sow buttons on a white sheet for yer man here!" said Mary Ellen, as she linked arms with Mucker.

"What about yerself, Mary Ellen, have ye everything ye need?" asked Martha.

"If Ah haven't by now Martha Ah'll never have," said Mary Ellen, "there's that much stuff in my bottom drawer sure the bottom will be falling out of it!"

"Well when yer up in The Square tomorrow call

into the Nugent Arms and book the reception and tell them I'll be in to settle up with them," said Martha.

"Ah'll see yis tomorrow," said Bobby as Mucker and Mary Ellen left arm-in-arm to walk out to Marlfield. Mucker was pleased with how the evening had went and how Bobby had engaged. He was beginning to feel confident that his plan would set Bobby on a more positive course and he could tell by the way Martha and Winnie had reacted that they also detected a change in his mood.

Mulling over such thoughts he walked on quietly with Mary Ellen. It was one of those calm, breathless nights on the Lough where a hush had descended. There was a silver moon in the sky dropping its flickering reflection into the Lough and casting ghostly shadows around Audley's Castle. They passed the Slip where the Auld Dog was now tied up. John McCluskey had kindly pumped it out and refloated it and in the moonlight it looked like an old battered silver galleon. Mucker felt a pang of sadness in his heart just looking at it. He could hear the Captain's voice in his head, 'A happy crew's a good crew,' ' The Auld Dog for the hard road,' and he recalled those happy days singing all the way to the Isle of Man. He felt like going down and sitting in it but decided to walk on. Mary Ellen sensed his hesitation:

"What are ye going to do with the Auld Dog, Mucker?" she said quietly.

"Ah dunno yet," said Mucker, "Ah'll probably be farming more than fishing now."

He was probably right as Mary Ellen's cousin, Nigel, had agreed to sell her his small farm. He had been waiting to see what was in aul' Dan's Will but when he was bequeathed no more land, there was no point trying to make a living out of it. On the other hand the two small farms combined would be a viable concern for Mucker and Mary Ellen starting their married life together and he was looking forward to a fresh start.

The next afternoon they met up with Bobby in The Square and went into Lawson's. It was a large ornate building with the Men's Department on the third floor. There was a long mahogany counter where rolls of material were being unfurled and cut to size and at the far end of the room there were tailors making the material into bespoke suits. This was where the gentlemen of the town came to be dressed - it was not the natural abode of the shoremen. Bobby had never been inside Lawson's before and Mucker could only remember being in once with Winnie when he was a boy. They were approached by a small well-dressed man with a tape-measure around his neck.

"Well how can I help you?" he said smiling.

"Have ye any light blue material for suits?" said Mucker smiling back at him.

"Light blue?" he replied thinking that he must have misheard what Mucker had said.

"Aye, light blue," repeated Mucker, "it's the whole go nowadays!"

"No, we don't have light blue, we have navy blue, black, brown, light grey, dark grey and olive green for something a bit different, all in checks or plain."

"So no light blue then?" continued Mucker.

"Well, I don't think it would suit our climate," said the shop assistant becoming slightly irritated.

"Ah well ye wouldn't know now unless ye stocked it," concluded Mucker. Mary Ellen decided it was time to intervene:

"We're not looking for suits, we're looking for shirts, ties and shoes."

"Well, you've come to the right place then – what size and colour of shoes?" Mucker was about to say 'light blue' but Bobby got in first:

"Shiny black shoes!" And the shiny black shoes in the right sizes were quickly produced and set down on the counter.

"And shirts?

"Yes, white shirts," said Mary Ellen, and the shop-assistant who had been dying to use his tape-measure since they came in, started to take Mucker and Bobby's neck and chest measurements and the shirts were also duly produced.

"Now ties, what colour are the suits?"

"Light blue!" said Mary Ellen trying not to laugh.

"Well, we've got navy blue, black, brown, light grey, dark grey and olive green ties."

"Do ye have them in checks?" asked Mucker.

"No, just plain. I would recommend navy blue as it would lift the suit."

"Well it wouldn't be the first time they've been lifted!" whispered Mucker to Bobby.

With business completed the shop assistant very quickly and efficiently cut a length of brown paper from a big roll at the end of the counter and a length of white string that hung down from the ceiling. The shirts and ties were carefully folded and packaged and the shoes likewise.

"Can we leave them here for now?" said Mary Ellen, "and mark them up for Mrs. Gibson who'll be in to collect them."

"Yes, that's fine," said the shop assistant. He stood smiling until they left the shop and then shook his head:

"Light blue suits! Whatever next – coloured underpants!"

The Nugent Arms was just across the street and architecturally could hold its own with any of the other buildings in the town. Bobby had delivered fish and lobsters to the kitchens on many occasions but had never just walked in the front door. He was more than impressed with the plush interior. This was where the gentlemen of the town went to relax, to have a drink or a meal, and to entertain friends and business acquaintances.

The head barman was Jamesy McMullan who, as it happened, was also a shoreman. His father and brothers were all sailors and fishermen but Jamesy had ignored the calling of the sea. 'The only wise one amongst us,' his father would say, quietly proud that his youngest son had done well in his chosen profession. Jamesy was a rarity among the shoremen – he didn't like the taste of alcohol. For this reason alone he was much sought after as a barman as he would never be sampling the stock or taking his work home with him. With such credentials he had risen to the position of head barman in the finest hotel in town.

But he was still a shoreman through and through and Mucker liked dealing with his own people rather than smiling shop assistants. Jamesy greeted them heartily being equally happy to be welcoming shore folk to the hotel for a change. Mary Ellen explained that they were hoping to book their wedding reception in the hotel next Friday but had still to finalise the numbers.

"Well if yer booking here, Mary Ellen, I think yer entitled to a wee complimentary drink," said Jamesy and in no time at all two bottles of stout and a sweet sherry were on the table beside them.

"I'll tell ye this, Mary Ellen," continued Jamesy, "on the day get the womenfolk to bring a few bottles in their handbags. The drink here is the same as Hannigan's but twice as dear and sure I'll turn a blind eye!"

Mucker smiled to himself as he took the first sip of his stout thinking to himself once a shoreman always a shoreman. Jamesy took his notebook and pen from his waistcoat pocket and handed them to Mary Ellen.

"Here, Mary Ellen, scribble away on that and when

yer ready I'll take the details," said Jamesy as he returned to the bar to serve another customer.

The usual suspects who would definitely be going to the wedding were quickly rounded up and accounted for in Jamesy's notebook. Mary Ellen conscious of involving Bobby in all the arrangements asked him if there was anyone, in particular, that he would like to see invited.

"Ah think ye should invite the Swails' and McDonalds' from Killard," said Bobby, "my Mammy really wants to meet Mrs. Swail to thank her for helping me."

"That's a great idea Bobby," said Mary Ellen, "and I'm sure we can get word to them easily enough."

"What about the Sergeant and Constable?" continued Bobby. Mary Ellen flashed a look at Mucker but saw that he was in total agreement. The Constable's words, that the Sergeant was his only friend here, had always stuck in his mind and Mucker was never one to refuse the hand of friendship, it wasn't the way of the shore people. There was no stopping Bobby now, he was on a roll.

"What about Steady Eddie?" he suggested.

"Wouldn't it be great if we could get him, Mucker," said Mary Ellen, "with him and aul' Ned sure the singing and dancing would be mighty!"

"Ah'll put the word out," said Mucker, "and see if anyone is fishing or whatever near the Isle of Man next week. He'd jump at the chance of coming over if he could."

With that Jamesy came over and sat down beside them. He took his notebook and pen which now seemed to contain all the information he needed.

"I was talking to the Head Chef," said Jamesy, "he was suggesting turkey and ham lunch and salmon for those who preferred fish."

This suggestion met with everyone's approval, in fact, turkey was quite exotic as duck or goose were still the birds of choice even at Christmas.

"Well where are yis for now?" said Jamesy as he saw them to the door.

"We're going out to see Father McAleenan," said Mary Ellen, "we probably should have confirmed the date with him first but there's no other weddings coming up, so I'm sure it'll be alright."

"Well, if there's any change sure just let me know," said Jamesy.

Leaving the Nugent Arms they strolled down the Big Back Lane and up the Windmill Hill towards the chapel that sat snugly in the hollow at the bottom of the hill. The view from the top of the Windmill Hill of Lough Cuan surging through the Narrows and out into the Irish Sea was always worth the climb. It had a certain magnetism, as even locals who had gazed upon it countless times, still stood and stared at a scene that could only have been created by the hand of God. The dismal winter was slowly giving way to spring. The birdsong had increased and the hawthorn hedgerows were beginning to leaf and bud in preparation for a covering of white blossoms that would lift everyone's spirits.

Father McAleenan was getting repairs done to the chapel roof and they found him talking to the builders when they arrived. Amid some banging and hammering from above they sat down in a pew at the back of the chapel. Mary Ellen explained that they were hoping to get married next Friday at twelve o'clock and Father McAleenan was more than willing to oblige.

"Have you known each other long?" he said smiling, being fully aware of their long courtship.

"About fifty years!" said Bobby.

"Och now Bobby," replied Father McAleenan.

"It seems like it sometimes," laughed Mary Ellen.

"The builders will be out this week," said Father McAleenan, "so we'll be well cleared up by Friday. I saw you at the Holy Hour on Sunday, Bobby, how are you keeping?"

"Bessy Murray says it should be called the Holy Hour and a Half," said Bobby. Father McAleenan laughed he always enjoyed how Bobby truthfully said whatever came into his head.

"Now, if I said that to her Bobby, she would deny it and then ask me to forgive her for telling lies in confession!"

"Ah, ye can't win Father," said Mucker laughing.

"Indeed not Mucker!"

"Do ye think the Captain's in Heaven, Father?" said Bobby out of the blue.

"Why do you ask Bobby?" said Father McAleenan

"Well he always wanted to be buried with a bottle of brandy for St. Peter but he never got his last wish," replied Bobby.

"In the gospel Bobby, Matthew says that whatever is done on earth shall be done in Heaven. And you know he has been supplying me with altar wine for years and sometimes a wee bottle of brandy, purely for medicinal purposes," he said in the direction of Mary Ellen and Mucker.

"Of course Father," said Mucker piously, trying to make Mary Ellen laugh.

"So Bobby what he has done on earth will be recognised in Heaven. But just to be sure I'll put a good word in for him as I'm on fairly good terms with the Man up above, you know!"

Although Father McAleenan had spoken light-heartedly he was unaware that he had lifted a considerable weight off Bobby's shoulders. He was sure now that the Captain was in Heaven with his father and for Bobby everything was right with the world.

With their business now all successfully completed they made their way back down to the shore to tell Martha how they had got on. Bobby couldn't wait to tell his mother what Father McAleenan had said.

"Well, didn't Ah tell ye that, Bobby," said Martha.

"You see ye should listen to yer mother,' began Mucker, "ye know Martha a good sally-rod along the back of the legs wud do that boy no harm!"

"Why don't ye shut yer big gub, Mucker," said

Bobby retaliating.

"Hey Bobby, wud ye come up to Hannigan's with me on Thursday night. It's my last night of freedom," said Mucker.

"Aye why not?" said Bobby, who could turn from foe to friend with Mucker in the blink of an eye. Mary Ellen and Martha smiled at one another knowing that normal service had been resumed and they got on with making the tea.

15 THE WEDDING

Bobby had not been in Hannigan's since the tragic boating accident and he was looking forward to going when Mucker called on the Thursday evening.

"Well are ye all ready for tomorrow, Mucker?" asked Martha.

"Aye, I've been ready for a while now, Martha," replied Mucker.

"Here Bobby take yer coat for it'll be caul' when ye get out," said Martha handing him his coat.

"Och we'll not be long Martha," said Mucker, "we're only going in for one."

When Mucker and Bobby approached Hannigan's they could hear the unmistakable voice of Steady Eddie:

I wish I was in Portaferry
Only for nights in Ballyhenry Bay…

Bobby was going to rush in but Mucker stopped him: "Just listen for a moment Bobby."

Eddie's song was being carried on the soft evening breeze out into the Lough. As the sound swirled in the air Mucker looked up at the night sky where a million stars seemed to be glistening and listening. After the last few weeks with aul' Dan, the Captain and Bobby this was a rare moment of reflection for Mucker. Almost for the first time he realised that after all these years he would be getting married in the morning.

"You know Bobby, Ah couldn't be marrying a better woman than Mary Ellen."

"And she couldn't be marrying a better man than you, Mucker!" replied Bobby, who at times, had the knack of saying exactly the right thing.

Mucker slapped him on the back and they went inside just as Eddie was finishing his song. There was a huge round of applause for Eddie which only increased in volume with the arrival of Bobby and Mucker. Eddie immediately embraced them and they sat down by the fire. Bobby failed to even notice that Eddie had taken up the Captain's seat.

"Ye made it then Steady," said Mucker.

"Aye, I'm staying in Tommy's tonight and tomorrow night and out on the first tide on Saturday morning," said Eddie.

"Is yer wife over?" asked Mucker.

"Nah, she doesn't like boats at the best of times and after what happened to the Captain, God rest him, there was no chance. And how are you now Bobby ?" asked Eddie.

"Ah'm grand Steady and better for seeing you," replied Bobby.

"There was a man asking for ye in the Isle of Man," continued Eddie winking at Mucker.

"And who was that?"

"It was Big Billy!"

"Sure the Captain said if Ah'd hit him Ah wud have knocked him into next week!" said Bobby.

"Well he'd have to get by me first," said Mucker, "so ye might never get landing that knock-out blow, Bobby."

At that Tommy arrived with three drinks. Although they had only intended having one drink but with having to celebrate Eddie's return to Portaferry, Bobby's return to Hannigan's and Mucker's wedding, the drinks continued to flow all night. It was the early hours of the morning before Mucker and Bobby returned home but as they were used to drinking late and getting up early, making the wedding for twelve o'clock the next day still felt like a lie in.

The morning of the wedding dawned as pleasant as could be expected for the time of year. Mucker had hired Andy McCormick to take Mary Ellen and her bridesmaid to and from the chapel.

"And no wee odd jobs in between Andy,' Mucker had warned, "Ah don't want to see dung or a dead calf in the back of the trap!"

"As if Ah wud!" said Andy.

"Ah know ye wud," said Mucker, "and don't be blowing that pipe smoke all round her either!"

Bobby and Mucker in their light blue suits, shiny black shoes, white shirts and navy blue ties, which lifted the suits, made their way out to the chapel with Martha, Wullie and Winnie. Mucker had also jokingly warned Mary Ellen to be on time as he had already waited long enough for her. And they were not long seated at the front of the chapel when Andy delivered Mary Ellen unscathed and on time. By the time the last bell had tolled the chapel was full and Father McAleenan emerged, thanked everyone for attending, and proceeded with the wedding ceremony without further ado.

"A reading from the gospel according to Mark: I will give you the keys to the Kingdom of Heaven; whatever you bind on earth shall be bound in Heaven…"

He looked down at Bobby as he spoke from the pulpit and Bobby knew exactly what the words meant. Most of the congregation, it should be said, were not really listening as their thoughts had drifted to the grubbing and drinking that lay before them at the Nugent Arms. Undaunted, Father McAleenan continued and safely negotiated the wedding vows and they were now on the home straight:

"If any person knows why this man and woman should not be joined in Holy Matrimony, let them speak now or forever hold their peace."

Bobby was probably the first to hear the exterior chapel door opening and what he thought was the familiar sound of wood tapping on the tiled floor. He glanced over his shoulder just as the interior door opened and there in the light that was streaming through the stained glass windows stood the Captain in a light blue suit. There was an audible gasp from the congregation as he made his way to the front of the chapel. Bobby who had been brought up to never talk in the chapel couldn't contain himself:

"Good on ye, Captain, good on ye!" he shouted and the whole congregation stood up and started to applaud.

When the Captain made it to the altar he exchanged words of congratulations with Mary Ellen and shook hands with Mucker who felt him slip something into his palm. When he opened his hand he saw that it was the old blackened penny that had been half way round the world. 'It's been lucky for me Mucker,' he whispered. He then put his arm firmly round Bobby's shoulder and said quietly 'Ah'm glad ye made it Bobby!' and for once Bobby was speechless.

The noise and excitement eventually abated and Father McAleenan, who was as elated as everyone else, could at last speak and be heard:

"I think that's what you call making an entrance

and I only hope that Jesus gets as warm a welcome when he returns. No doubt there is a story behind what you've just witnessed but it'll have to wait.

"Now Captain I take it that you have no objections to this couple being joined in Holy Matrimony?"

"None whatsoever Father I fully endorse it," said the Captain in his familiar husky tone that no one present thought that they would ever hear again.

With the wedding ceremony concluded the wedding party went with Father McAleenan into the vestry to sign the register. The congregation spilled out into the morning sunshine with the buzz of excitement almost palpable. Some of the devout chapel-goers thought that they had maybe witnessed a miracle and were unsure if the Captain would re-emerge or if they had just seen an apparition. But emerge he did and to prevent him being mobbed Mucker bundled him into Andy's trap with Mary Ellen and her bridesmaid bound for the Nugent Arms.

In the crowd Bobby found Mrs. Swail and introduced her to his mother. Martha thanked her profusely for the assistance she had rendered Bobby.

"Och he never stopped calling out for ye Mrs. Gibson. Mind you, I don't think he liked my fish soup, but that's the boy to get ye on yer feet!" said Mrs. Swail.

"Ah got on my feet to get away from it," joked Bobby.

"Do ye hear him Mrs. Swail sure the young ones

now don't know what's good for them. He says the same about the buttermilk," said Martha.

And so enjoying criticising the younger generation, as the older generation always did, they made their way happily to the hotel. The grubbing and drinking that had occupied many thoughts during the wedding ceremony was now the reality. And the Nugent Arms had never witnessed such a capacity for drinking and eating and for the revelry that followed. Aul' Ned was belting out the tunes on the fiddle, Eddie and others were up singing, Bobby was dancing and the Captain was telling his story to anyone who would listen – which was everyone!

"… when Ah set Bobby aff for Killard Ah thought he was trying to swim it underwater Ah had forgot all about the coins in his pockets. The Routen Wheel then spat me out but instead of drifting to Killard Ah was caught in the flow going out over the Bar.

"Mind you I was floating fairly well on the bit of stern but my leg was so caul' Ah was glad that Ah only had one of them. After about an hour here didn't Ah see the Portavogie fishing fleet heading out.

"Ah let a roar out of me that the wind must have caught as one of the fleet veered aff towards me. It was Captain Cully, 'Is that you, Captain?' says he, 'It is," says I, 'Wud ye be looking a lift?' says he, 'Ah'd be much obliged,' Ah replied.

"So they got me on board, warmed me up and dried me out. They were heading out fishing aff Scotland so Ah said Ah wud give them a hand as the least Ah cud do. So we were fishing and landing the catch round Scotland until we got stranded up in the Shetlands when a storm set in and we were stuck there for a while.

"Anyway, Ah only got into Strangford this morning and by the way folk were looking at me you wud have thought Ah had risen from the dead. Ah heared someone on the ferry say that Mucker was getting married so Ah made it to Hannigan's. Andy was sitting there having a wee half 'un so Ah got the suit on me and he ran me out to the chapel. So here Ah am large as life and twice as ugly as they say.

"Mind you," said the Captain in a more serious tone, "Ah had time to think when we were stuck in Scotland and Ah've decided to retire from the sea as Ah've used up my nine lives, maybe more. Tommy and I have a few business ideas that'll keep me busy and stop me from falling into the sea." Everyone seemed to agree that the Captain was making the right decision

The Captain had been sitting at a table with Eddie and Tommy and conversing with a constant stream of well-wishers expressing their delight at his return. Martha had insisted that he would be getting his money back but the Captain was equally insistent that he wouldn't as it was Bobby's future and eventually Martha accepted his argument.

Eddie had now been called for the final song and Tommy was getting the drinks in and the Captain for the first time had a quiet moment to himself. He looked round and saw Mucker and Mary Ellen happily married at last, Bobby and Martha with enough to see them through many a hard winter, Eddie happy as a lark at being back in Portaferry and the Sergeant and Constable talking excitedly to old Sergeant Berry about their forthcoming promotions. His stream of thought was interrupted when Tommy returned with the drinks:

"A penny for them, Captain," said Tommy.

"Ah was just thinking Tommy it's true what they say - a rising tide lifts all boats!'

"Yer right there, Captain. And it'll be lifting Steady back to the Isle of Man in the morning," said Tommy. Eddie was finishing with the song he always ended with:

> So fill to me the parting glass
> And drink a health whate'er befall
> Then gently rise and softly call
> Good night and joy be to you all...

ALSO BY THE SAME AUTHOR

Us Boys In Portaferry

Away And Play Round Yer Own Dures

Us Boys And The Portaferry Banshee

Digging Up the Past In Ballyphilip Churchyard

Around Portaferry In 80 Poems

Standing On The Shoulders Of Giants: A History Of Portaferry Football (co-author with M. McMullan)

Printed in Great Britain
by Amazon